Reading
BOROUGH COUNCIL

Reading Borough Libraries

Email: info@readinglibraries.org.uk
Website: www.readinglibraries.org.uk

D1187121

TEL: 0118 901 5109

- 4 JAN 1993   12. 05.

19. OCT   25. OCT   18. SEP 04
21. JAN. 03.   02. DEC 04

02. NOV   06. SEP 03.   RESV
16. DEC 03.   12. MAY 08
14. FEB 02   23. JAN 04   - 2 AUG 2018

23. FEB 02.   17. FEB 04.

12. APR 02   10. JUN 04.
13. AUG 04.
01. OCT 02   31. AUG 04.

19. OCT   MAR 00

CLASS NO. A/GW

TO AVOID FINES THIS BOOK SHOULD BE RETURNED ON
OR BEFORE THE LAST DATE STAMPED ABOVE, IF NOT
REQUIRED BY ANOTHER READER IT MAY BE RENEWED BY
PERSONAL CALL, TELEPHONE OR POST, QUOTING THE
DETAILS DISPLAYED.

OCT 1988

0715 622 692 1 002 X2

THE SKELETON
IN THE CUPBOARD

THE SKELETON
IN THE CUPBOARD

Alice Thomas Ellis

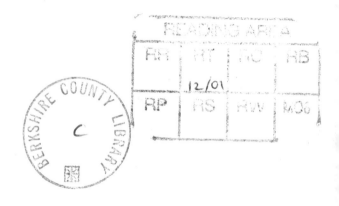

READING AREA

| RM | RT | RC | RB |
| RP | RS | RW | RWC |

12/01

BERKSHIRE COUNTY LIBRARY

C

Duckworth

First published in 1988 by
Gerald Duckworth & Co. Ltd.
The Old Piano Factory
43 Gloucester Crescent, London NW1

© 1988 by Alice Thomas Ellis

All rights reserved. No part of this
publication may be reproduced, stored in a
retrieval system, or transmitted, in any
form or by any means, electronic, mechanical,
photocopying, recording or otherwise, without
the prior permission of the publishers.

ISBN 0 7156 2269 2

British Library Cataloguing in Publication Data

Ellis, Alice Thomas *1932–*
The skeleton in the cupboard.
Rn: Anna Haycraft   I. Title
823'.914 [F]

ISBN 0-7156-2269-2

SOUTHCOTE
─ OCT 1988

Photoset in North Wales by
Derek Doyle & Associates, Mold, Clwyd.
Printed in Great Britain by
Billing & Sons Limited, Worcester.

I hadn't given her a thought for years. I had had no reason to think about her – not really. I was old Mrs Monro and my life was over.

Monica called one morning to ask if I wanted anyone else put on the guest list and said, as though it didn't matter, that *she* was coming to stay for the wedding. She said '*Lili*'s coming', and I put my cup down very carefully in its saucer. It was winter and I was cold. I could see my fingers trembling and put my hands in the pockets of my cardigan. Winter gets worse as you get older.

'Have some more coffee, Monica,' I said. 'Are they back then?' I remembered the relief when they had left. It was years before, but I still remembered the relief.

She said, 'Robert has an exhibition arranged. They'll be staying for a few weeks.'

'A few weeks,' I said. 'How nice.' I poured her another cup of coffee and put my hands back in my pockets.

At some point my flesh had ceased to be of much significance to me, and it was my bones of which I was always conscious. My bones were cold and they ached, perhaps to remind me that before too long they would be all that remained of me: the neglected skeleton's revenge, as the pampered flesh decayed away. I was reflecting thus gloomily because I was unfairly enraged with Monica, and spite and unhappiness frequently go together. I could not reach over and slap her for bringing Lili back into my life, but I could break a less stringent social taboo and embarrass her with talk of my age and impending death. I could remark reflectively, 'I suppose, after all, we are all only skeletons in our own cupboards, waiting to be revealed.' That'd serve her right, I thought, but I kept silent. Such subtle aggression would be wasted on Monica. She would respond with some bromide and make me even crosser. Years had gone by since I'd been able to say things as they came into my head, knowing that I should be understood. The people who would have understood had all gone away. Sometimes I made Syl laugh, but he was my son and it was different. I had missed those who had been my friends for so long now that deprivation had become my element. I had adapted like some Darwinian prototype to loneliness and now could never revert to what I had been. I was sorry for myself, but I would have died rather than let anybody know. Dislike was preferable to pity since people mostly dislike from a distance. They seldom bother to come to you in order to dislike you, whereas pity brings them thronging, eager to express this gratifying emotion and gain whatever is to be gained of credit – in time and eternity. I had not, of course, always been so cynical.

*

When Monica left I went into the sitting-room and sat down. The dog was looking at me, lying with paws outstretched, his eyes filmed and bulging. Syl had brought him for me when Jack died, so he was an old dog now. I hadn't wanted a dog, especially not a small, peculiar pug, but Syl's fiancée's bitch had just had a litter and Syl had thought a puppy would be company for me. He had fully intended marrying the girl, although no date had been set, and his father's death had come at an inconvenient time. How could he marry when his mother had just been widowed? He and the girl came with the puppy and a mushroom basket for it to sleep in until we made more permanent arrangements. That particular girl was, in my view, too sweet to be wholesome. She would look at me with brimming eyes, rather like the dog, and bring me exasperating posies from her mother's garden – little bits of flowers and leaf and twig tied up with shiny ribbon. She would catch my eye with her brimming one and glare into it with deep compassion. I used to long to say how pleasant a change it was to be widowed, and watch her expression alter, but I had learned over many years to be guarded and to control my inclinations. Besides, Syl seemed fond of her. He fussed around her, as though she were made of porcelain, and it was already high time he was married, being well into his thirties.

Time: it seemed I could think of nothing else. So much had passed, and still it flew. It must be running out for me, but I went on, seemingly indestructible: a little bored but not unbearably so. I began thinking more and more about the past, and had to make an effort to return to the present. I would come back from the moors of my youth still feeling the wind in my hair and catch a glimpse of an old woman in the darkened windows. Looking in the mirror I could see no trace of the girl whose life I had been reliving. Old age seemed to me not so much a natural progression as a disguise: a suit of unsuitable clothes, ill-fitting and inappropriate. I fell into the habit of sadness and gave up the practice of hope. It made existence easier.

'I have a lamb's kidney for you, dog,' I said, and he

7

got to his feet, shaking slightly. When he was a pup I had kept treading on him; whether it was his fault or mine I could never determine. He had squealed 'Pen and ink, pen and ink', and Syl's fiancée would leap to console him – 'Who's a poor little baby, then?' All in all I was more glad than regretful when that engagement ended. Syl grew very white and quiet, and I know he telephoned her in the night to ask her to come back to him. She never did, not once, and I used to wonder why. Then after a few weeks he fell in love again. He never had any trouble finding girls.

I went to the kitchen and got the kidney from the larder. 'Soon, dog,' I said, 'soon, soon', as I sliced it up into small bits for his old teeth and his old gums.

He found it difficult to chew and his breath smelled, but I felt I was in no position to criticise. I was, as they say, no oil painting myself. I had never liked him as much as a dog should be liked, and now it was too late. I had never quite been able to dissociate him from his origins and the fleeing fiancée. Even now he reminded me of loss. That he had arrived at the time of Jack's death did not worry me. I had never liked Jack as much as a husband should be liked.

Considering this, I bent down and patted the dog as he snuffled the bits of kidney. My back ached as I straightened up, and he snarled briefly at me.

'You're an ungrateful little swine, dog,' I told him, 'and the world is too cold a place for you to bite the hand that feeds you.'

I had had a sheep-dog once who had leapt across the moors, his hair sleeked by the facing wind. I had gone home with him to golden fires, and sometimes I thought that all I retained of warmth and joy – and it was now little enough – had been stored up in those days and seldom since replenished. My memories of youth were of movement and life, of cold wind, bracken-and-gorse-scented, fire and a warmth of summer more significant in the North, more notable than it could be in a gentler climate. The clear air had seemed to clarify everything – sentiments and sensation.

I went back to the sitting-room and the dog followed. Syl had had the end part of the house converted for me, so that when he married I should be out of the way of the bride. I had suggested that there was nothing to prevent him from buying his own house but he had not seemed to listen. I was not blind to Syl's faults. He could be spontaneously and ridiculously generous, but he was also mean. I could hardly blame him for this trait, since it was from me that he got his Yorkshire blood and Yorkshiremen are known the world over as careful.

I was not delighted to be consigned to only a part of my own house, but I didn't care enough to argue about it. One of my anxieties was that I knew Syl would spend a good deal of his time with me in my new quarters and Margaret would be left rattling round on her own in the rest of the house. I had ceased to wonder why Syl not only stayed with me but sought out my company. It had become very noticeable when his father died and I had tried once or twice then to tell him that he need not trouble himself about me – I was quite self-sufficient. Again he had not seemed to listen, and in the end I was forced to accept that, for some reason, he would stay with me. I knew it would appear to everyone that I was a possessive and demanding mother, but I didn't care. There was very little I could do about it. Some of the girls had complained that he spent more time with me than he did with them, but Syl could be stubborn. I also think that he believed he could have everything. He had

9

always wanted everything – both sorts of cake at tea-time, jelly *and* blancmange at parties – when he was a child. It didn't seem like greed – more like curiosity. I used to wonder if that was why he had so many girls. He was not truly an amorist since he always meant the latest girl to be the last, believing her to be finally the love of his life. Then she would run away – and I never did understand that – or Syl would tire of her, and look around for another source of sweetness. Or perhaps I mean a sort of sweetmeat.

I had not yet used the converted part of the house, despite all the trouble Syl had taken to make it pleasant. I was waiting until Margaret moved in. Margaret.

*

When she left school she stayed at home all day. I used to walk the dog along the path bordering the golf course and I would see her, most mornings, sitting in the summer-house – sometimes reading, sometimes just staring into space. It seemed unnatural. When I was your age, I would say to her in my mind, I was preparing to go to college. I did not say in my mind what I really remembered: when I was your age I was in love, I was alive. That is not the kind of thing the old say to the young.

I had not seen her very often as she grew up because she was sent away to school. I remember that she always seemed to be at home during the holidays, for I found it strange. She never brought a friend home with her and whenever I came across her she was on her own. Most girls of her age spent at least part of their holidays in each other's houses, went around in packs or in pairs and lounged a lot – like wild cats – before marriage and responsibility domesticated them and dulled their shining fur, silenced their wails. Adolescence is usually typified by an unanswerable combination of innocence and insolence. As their elders require that they should conform to society's demands, to the hypocrisy – if we are to be honest – that makes life possible, the young often respond with a curious superiority. It is unlikely that they have yet done anything truly dreadful and they suspect that their elders probably have. To be told how to behave by a person steeped in moral turpitude is annoying to everyone, but more particularly to the young. And then the old grow exasperated by the stupidity of the young: by their failure to realise that moral decline is a matter only of time, and that as circumstances alter they too will be forced to cut corners and compromise their early – and unfortunately vague – ideals. Of course only the good die young. With a few rare exceptions only the young *are* good. Margaret sometimes struck me as too good to be true. She had not that quality of fresh and honest surprise and indignation that I have been speaking of. Rather she had a copybook conformity which only a fool could have taken for the real thing. The real virtue of youth lies in that impulsive generosity, and Margaret was as contained and closed and mute as her mother's meat safe. On the face of it she was the perfect girl: obedient, disciplined, quiet, sober and undemanding, and yet she was wholly unnatural. Perhaps Syl was deceived by her appearance, by the way she behaved like a much older person, into imagining that she was unusually mature for her age. No, he wasn't. He found her similar to me, and also might have thought that behind her reserve lay those much-vaunted banked fires beloved of novelists. I've never believed in them myself. Ice and fire do not

11

co-exist and all the romantic longing in the world will not make it so.

Monica was caught in the common trap between parental fondness and exasperation. When people enquired over the tea table what Margaret was going to do now I could see her torn between snapping 'Nothing' and explaining that Margaret was resting after the rigours of school before deciding between a career in the diplomatic corps or a suitable marriage. I recognised her dilemma, for Syl, while his problems were different from Margaret's, caused me similar feelings of irritation. One of the reasons I was seeing fewer and fewer people was that I was sick and tired of being called on to explain why Syl was yet unmarried. 'Mind your own damned business' is the response of those who are aggrieved because they have something to hide. I had evolved an air designed to give the impression that I could not understand their question, that to me there was nothing untoward in Syl's condition. In truth, of course, no one wondered more searchingly about it than I. My sisters-in-law, all of whom had grandchildren, had become particularly unwelcome to me as time passed. From resentment of Syl's undoubted beauty as a child to envy of his achievement in passing his law exams with honours, they had progressed to a shared *Schadenfreude* at his failure to wed and breed. I frequently had an image, which visited me unbidden, of the backs of girls flouncing down the drive, never to return. Not the least worrying was the speed with which he recovered from these rejections.

Each sister-in-law, like a bad fairy, had a different form of words with which to attack me, from 'Syl not married *yet*? to 'How good of Syl to look after you so well', an implication that I was a monstrous mother, destroying her son's chance of a future, of fulfilment and happiness. I could not explain that there was nothing I wanted more than that Syl should leave me: go away and leave me alone. In a way I was protecting him by letting the world believe that his state was all my fault. It seemed preferable to the view that he was a hopelessly inadequate human being. My annoyance at being cast into this role was vitiated by my awareness that, like it or not, there was some truth in it. I did not like it at all. I did not care to remember that my own marriage had left much to be desired, that I had not married the man I loved and that when Syl had started to grow up I had indeed preferred his company to that of his father. Now I no longer needed company. I had had enough and I wanted to be left to think about things I had not had time to think about. Increasingly I remembered my childhood, the beginning: the dark spaces of the farmhouse, the endless moors and the perfection of smallness in the hawthorn, white with birth, bright with death. I thought more of winter than I did of summer. It seemed to me that those Northern moors were designed to receive snow; intended for the winds to pass untrammelled. Summer was a dull season. In spring things were growing; in autumn they were harvested; in winter they were waiting. Summer was pointless, designed for idleness. An inbred Yorkshire puritanism led me to despise it. I wondered why I was thinking of summer with winter all around me.

It was the egg sandwiches that reminded me. Shaking white pepper into the mashed egg, I was back in a more recent past than the one I habitually roamed: only about fifteen years ago, which is nothing. It was cold in the pantry. I had chosen this house because it was just a

13

little like the stone-built houses of the North, of my childhood. Jack had favoured a more exotic residence which had also been on sale just up the road, but I put my foot down. There were some things I could be stubborn about, and I refused to live in a house designed, as far as I could tell, on the lines of a Dutch dairy. Jack had decided that we should retire to this neighbourhood, indeed to this particular road. One of the firm's bosses had lived and died here. Something about this ill-expressed, incoherent estate represented worldly success to Jack, and I didn't really care enough to question the assumption.

Derek and Monica had shared his view and followed us here. Certainly you had to be well-off to be able to afford the absurd buildings that rose like apparitions on either side of the private road. Manifestations of architectural fantasy appeal to those who know no better. I never said this to Jack. There would have been no point. I was undoubtedly a snob in some matters but I kept silence. Jack had been dismayed by my uncles' farmhouse. I had (only to give him the benefit of the doubt) taken him there once when we were first married and its charm had escaped him. He was town-bred, the son of a cotton broker, and his aspirations were formed by the views of his father and his father's contemporaries. 'I don't know much about art but I know what I like and I've got t'brass to pay for it' was their attitude. I was never an aesthete, but I did not care for pastiche. The house in which I would end my days stood amongst a medley of wildly assorted historical and geographical styles, and I missed the assurance of roots, of houses built of local stone, of people speaking in the accents of the district. I had been homesick for most of my life. Inevitably I would have

14

little in common with the others who had chosen to live here. I was a fish out of water. When Derek came back from Egypt bringing Monica and the baby I was not enthralled. He was some sort of distant cousin of Jack's, although much younger, and worked for the same shipping firm. There was a tendency in the North for relations to work in the same firm. They liked each other no more than relations anywhere but they stuck together. I used to think it was a kind of tribal imperative in face of threat from the South. Jack, who, to be fair, was not entirely stupid, said once that they would be company for me, friends from our days in Liverpool, but he didn't repeat it. Derek was cast in much the same mould as Jack, so he was the wrong sort of Northerner for me. I wondered whether North and South married more easily than Town and Country, yet that was absurd, for I had left the country when I went to college and I had never been a rustic. Perhaps it was really very simple: I didn't love my husband, so I didn't like his house.

I sneezed, startling the dog who was hoping something might drop from the pantry shelf into his waiting mouth. The sneeze jarred me and I said 'Ouch'.

The dog sat looking at me and I felt foolish for speaking aloud to myself.

'How are *your* bones?' I asked him. 'You're as old as me. How do *you* feel?' Talking to the dog was in a more acceptable category than talking to oneself. 'Does your back ache when you sneeze?'

I stirred the pepper into the egg and started to butter the loaf. The dog, who had got up, sat down again, prepared to continue waiting. He wasn't interested in conversation at the moment. It was in the evening that he liked to be addressed occasionally, lying in front of the coal fire, dozing. Sometimes he had bad dreams.

15

'You eat too much,' I said to him as he watched me. 'On the other hand,' I said, 'I seem to be making too much tea for two.'

I put the sandwiches and cake on a tray, and the scones to warm in the oven. I think I hoped that Margaret, who was too thin, would be tempted to eat at least one of these offerings.

'You're too fat,' I said to the dog, who whined in response. 'I'm too old,' I said, like a character out of one of those serial fairy stories. 'And this pantry is cold.'

'Fee Fi Fo Fum,' I said under my breath and I knew how I would appear to an observer: an old woman muttering to herself. The old seemed always to look down and inwards, and speak, most of all, to themselves.

The smell of newly made egg sandwiches is not to be denied. It was again summer that I was reluctantly remembering now. I was already old fifteen years ago but my bones were holding up better. I was remarkable for my age, as they say: quite frisky in fact. Jack had not yet died. Syl was engaged to what is known as a 'nice girl', which meant, when analysed to its smallest components, that she was as boring as hell but at least she wasn't a whore. I recalled now with wry regret that I had thought her not good enough for Syl.

There had still seemed some point then in the round of dinners, ladies' lunches, teas, picnics, bridge parties which constituted what was known in my youth as social intercourse. Not a great deal of point – never that – but rather more than now. Now I was moving towards the grave and would give another dinner party only over my own dead body. Even the small suppers and teas to which I occasionally entertained Monica and one or two other acquaintances were taxing and boring in equal

16

proportion. If Syl would only leave home, I thought, I would never have to cook again. The dog and I could live on scraps and the contents of tins. But then I thought of the time a year or so before when I had fallen downstairs. Monica had come in through the back door calling my name. I had retained the custom of my childhood of not locking doors, and now I was rewarded. I heard her telling the ambulance men that she had found me lying there unconscious and icy cold and had telephoned them immediately. I'd come round by then, and on the whole I was rather annoyed. As I was saying, I was relieved to know that Syl was always around in case I should have an accident and lie helpless with broken bones but, having toppled downstairs and knocked myself out, it seemed quite pointless that at my age I should recover. I could have quietly faded into whatever comes next for the children of man, but as it was I had no more than a lump on the head and a black eye. I was doomed to go on going through the motions of life. Quite uselessly, it seemed to me, I was to live until I'd eaten more egg sandwiches.

How difficult it is to keep to the point when you grow old. Not only because the brain cells are failing but because there is so much to explain. So much unharnessed, uncategorised experience leads up to each new episode – no matter how trivial. Each new happening is not new, but an echo, a reminder, or a repetition of something that has happened before – and quite possibly before that, and before that again. Certainly I had eaten many egg sandwiches in my life.

As I carried the tray from the kitchen I thought of the last time Margaret and I had eaten egg sandwiches together. She must have been very small, since it was shortly after they had returned from Egypt and I had felt the odd wish which no other child (except Syl, of course, for whom as a baby I would have offered myself as a feast) had ever aroused in me, to cosset her. She seemed even then to be lacking something which was the birth-right of every child. I had no idea what it could be. She was well-dressed and, although tiny, clearly not undernourished, and her mother kept a constant eye on her. She was too quiet. Syl felt it as well. He kept offering her little bits of 'eggy samblidge. It'll make you grow up into a big girl.' 'No thank you,' Margaret would say. 'Anchovy samblidge,' Syl would offer. 'Little tiny fishes in it.' 'No thank you.' 'You'll never grow up to be a big girl. Don't you want to be a big girl?' 'No thank you.' Lili and Robert were staying with Monica and I had asked them all to tea in the garden. There were rugs on the lawn, and garden chairs, but Lili chose to perch on an overgrown, neglected rockery built over the old air-raid shelter because, she explained, she didn't want to ruin the lawn with her cigarette ends, and the rockery was conveniently full of little cracks and holes hidden by the wild grass which had seeded itself there. I could see her now. She was wearing white and her red hair stuck out all round her head.

Syl's fiancée was also making a fuss of Margaret. She had the air of a girl who believes that there is no prettier sight in the world than that of a young woman being kind to an innocent child. I never could be fair to that girl.

It was Lili who fascinated Margaret. She sat high on the rockery talking her nonsense and all the men hung round like flies. I had a feeling that she smoked so much in order to keep them at a certain distance. Then Margaret crawled up the slope to sit by her and I wondered at Lili's quality.

I lived too much in the past. I don't know why this should be considered reprehensible but I often resolved to cure myself of the habit and face the present. There was nothing too terrible about my life, no need to turn away from it or pretend it was other than it was. The truth is I was bored. I had not been bred to suburbia. I had not intended or imagined that I should end my days in a London suburb behind a screen of spotted laurels. I had never really expected to grow old. The wisdom that is supposed to come with age seemed to me only an accumulation of repeated experience, a realisation that people and their emotions are much alike. I found it irritating that, this being the case, no one was able or prepared to learn from the experience of others. I had watched many people go through the motions of birth, marriage and death convinced of the uniqueness of their experience and I could think of nothing to say to them. Congratulations always seemed to me premature, and when disaster struck commiserations were otiose. I went through the forms with less and less conviction and came to be perceived as begrudging, negative and, I suppose, sour, although I retained enough *amour propre* to feel somewhat reduced by that description. The world has always feared old women, witches. I had known some cheerful old people, but their lives had worked on them differently and I found them tiresome. The optimism of others is always irritating and appears peculiarly misplaced in the elderly. In view of the way the world is constituted it appears misplaced (although more forgivable) in the young as well. I remembered being hopeful. I remembered sliding on a frozen tarn as a tawny sun

19

retired obliquely behind a darkening hill, and the exhilaration of cold and shadow contrasting with my own warmth. I had sometimes felt what perhaps we should all feel always – that I was an integral part of everything, of everything that was huge and all that was small. Now I was part of hardly anything. I worried that Syl was aware of this. I worried more that he was using the evidence of my emptiness to excuse his own refusal to take any chances.

Margaret reminded me of myself. Not as I had been, but as I was. Syl fell in love with her. No one could understand why. She was very quiet and seemed to take no interest in anything, but I knew why. She was like me. Syl would need to learn no new lessons. She was not disruptive. She was not even remotely self-assertive. Also she was beautiful and unaware of it, and there is perhaps nothing so seductive as unselfconscious beauty. Yet I was always puzzled by Syl's attitude to her. I have to admit that, if I'm to be honest with myself. I had watched Jack when he was Syl's age making sheep's eyes at girls young enough to be his daughter and showing no signs of awareness of his own foolishness. I had thought that odd; had thought that even if he couldn't help himself and was compelled to behave like an ass, he should, at least, have shown some acknowledgment of his own ludicrous plight, a sheepish smile to go with the sheep's eyes perhaps, but he had been quite unaware of the effect he made.

Syl had never struck me as being as foolish as his father. I was prejudiced in his favour, and anyway his proclivities, even if they reflected badly on me as a mother, did not make me seem vicariously ridiculous as my husband's carryings on had done. With Syl I had never felt that common female compulsion to invert the soup tureen on a man's head as he goes into the old routine. Syl had begun by flirting with Margaret as he automatically flirted with any woman and I had been surprised – no, shocked – when he announced that he was yet again engaged to be married.

Of all the girls Margaret seemed to me the least likely as Syl's wife, or indeed as anybody's wife. Nubile, for some reason, was not a word one associated with Margaret. She had a cool clear quality and it was impossible to imagine her in a transport of passion. For one thing, she never giggled. Most of Syl's girls had giggled a good deal, and wriggled as well. Wriggling and giggling, regrettable as it seems, are the human female's means of indicating willingness to be courted, and Margaret had a curious dignity which was incompatible with sexuality.

I was never certain, to put it at its simplest, that Syl was really in love with her, because I couldn't see why he should be. I feared that perhaps vanity had led him to wish it to be known that he could still procure for himself young and beautiful women. He did care about her. He fussed around her and tried to give her treats, and sometimes I thought that what he really wanted was not a wife but a child.

He took her to Brighton one day, getting up early and spending some time with his head under the bonnet of his car, ensuring it would carry her safely. She was late, and Syl came into the house looking at his watch and wondering aloud what she was doing. After a while he went to fetch her, and when they came back I was standing in the doorway holding his sweater, since he had left it on the hall table and I didn't want him to forget it. It could turn cold by the sea. Something had made him very angry. He was white and his movements

21

were hurried and careless and he threw shut the open door of the car. Margaret was unperturbed. The last girl had grown supplicatory when Syl was angry: penitent and fearful. But Margaret looked at him as though she thought he was mad.

'She says she doesn't want to go,' Syl had told me – and to Margaret: 'Why didn't you tell me before?' 'I didn't think it was important,' said Margaret. 'I'll come with you,' I offered, trying to lighten the situation, and Margaret said in her clear voice with no hint of a remorseful tremor: 'I've agreed to go if you really want me to.' 'Too kind of you to *agree*,' Syl snarled, and I thought that if her small pedantries irritated him so much it boded ill for the future.

He was still in a rage when he got home. Or perhaps it was a fresh rage and they had had a pleasant day together. I never found out, since it would have been injudicious to ask. A few years earlier he could have taken her for donkey rides and bought her candy floss, and as I reflected on this I thought that the proposed marriage was the stupidest thing I'd ever heard of. She was too young for Syl and, to my own mortification, I found I was again thinking, too *good*. I examined this odd thought but could find no reason to reject it. Syl, much as I loved him, was an ordinary mortal and there was something strange about Margaret. Perhaps 'good' was not the word, but whatever the quality I had discerned in her it unsuited her for everyday human things and I could think of no appropriate uses to which she might put herself. I found it impossible to picture her pushing a pram.

*

The doorbell rang and the dog barked. I wished as usual that my visitor might have forgotten to come, but it was too late now. I opened the door, and although I was aware that Margaret was there all I could see was Lili. Of course I knew that they had arrived from Egypt, knew I would have to see her sooner or later, but not now. I was not over-zealous about the social niceties but I could have strangled Margaret for bringing her without warning. I was, for a moment, speechless.

Lili seemed not to have changed at all. I would describe her as garish, but that wouldn't be fair. She was vividly *alive*. A cartload of monkeys, I thought confusedly, and had a sudden halucinatory impression of the Blackpool Illuminations as I submitted to her kiss. Considering the circumstances under which we had last parted, I found her attitude remarkable, even admirable. Or perhaps she led such a varied life that she had thought the event of no significance. Perhaps she had no recollection of it. I found myself quite unable to behave naturally and fell back on convention, wondering as I offered egg sandwiches whether she would remember the garden picnic. Her behaviour then had been impeccable, and if, as seemed possible, she couldn't remember the outrageous things she had done later it seemed improbable that she would remember a small party of no interest or importance at all where she had done nothing untoward.

Margaret seemed paler and quieter than usual. She refused sandwiches and fiddled with a scone. I could still think of nothing to say to Lili and grew exasperated with Margaret for being so hopelessly little help. I think Lili too began to feel the constraint, for she accused the poor old dog of assaulting her foot. I would not myself have chosen quite this method of easing a social

23

situation but it was better than nothing. I had been on the point of screaming as Margaret made crumbs and looked as though she were waiting only for the tumbril to come and carry her off, while Lili gazed at me brightly as though wondering what had happened to my powers of conversation. I had always found her amusing – what Monica would have called 'stimulating company'. If she had not come unexpectedly I might have been able to cope, but as it was I could only gape.

I went to fetch more hot water for the teapot – unnecessarily since it was nearly full, but I had to do something. I stood in the kitchen and swore under my breath, determining to ask Lili what Egypt was like these days. It would surely make a more fruitful topic than the state of the crops, which was the only other thing I could think of. It didn't interest me at all, but then nothing did. As I realised this, I wondered why I wasn't bored when I was alone, and concluded with some surprise that, although by no stretch of the imagination could I call myself happy, I was content with myself and my own thoughts. I had not wondered about it before and no one had told me that this was one of the consolations of age. There weren't many.

I was extremely careful as I poured the boiling water into a jug, and careful as I walked back to the table. I had to be very cautious now of heat and height and distance. Ordinary things, all part of the world as it was made for humans, had become dangerous and threatening. Fires and steps and floors waited for me to pitch myself against them: not with malice, but with an unpleasant, alien patience. The world, it seemed, grew passively hostile as death loomed closer. I no longer felt at home in it. I had an impression that my frailty was somehow despicable, and that the forces of nature found me expendable. Looked at another way, this was undoubtedly true. The aged of other cultures have voluntarily lost themselves in forests or flung themselves off ice-floes when they have judged themselves to be of no further use. This purely utilitarian view has never struck me as totally unreasonable, even if a little harsh. Other people have paid great respect to their ancients and, considering myself, I thought it had probably been misplaced. I did not feel wise, just old. I have said before that the wisdom of age is merely an accumulation of experience. Repetitiveness is wearisome. Even Syl became impatient when I repeated myself, and I sometimes thought I could not bear to brush my hair once more. Now I hear myself saying again what I have said before, and find myself tiresome. Perhaps that is why the old mumble to themselves – out of consideration, not only for others, but for their own pride's sake. I must say, as I speak of pride, that I was never unintelligent. Intelligence is perhaps my favourite quality. There is something almost evil in real stupidity, and perhaps 'wisdom' is only a softer, larger, furrier word for the lithe, naked 'intelligence'.

I went reluctantly back to the tea table. Lili was intelligent and so, I believed, was Margaret, although she seldom gave evidence of it. Sometimes she would reveal an unsuspected wit, but then she would hastily cover it as though somebody might chide or punish her. I wished I knew what was wrong with her, what had so silenced her.

If only Lili would for God's sake say something which would keep my attention. I remembered her talking the hind leg off a donkey and how I had sometimes wished she'd shut up. That had been when I had something to say: before I'd said all I have to say again and again. She did give a brief description of the journey through Italy but she was not on her old form. Once, in these circumstances, I would have fetched a bottle of whisky to loosen her tongue, but I could myself no longer drink as I used to and I had come to realise that the only purpose of alcohol in an awkward social situation is to make the listeners less critical. The person holding the floor should ideally be stone cold sober since drink has never made anyone more amusing. It does greatly help though if the audience is half-seas over. Now in the evenings with my small glass of sherry I found the company unsurpassedly tedious as they waxed merry on their huge martinis, as their own jokes appeared to them to be rib-splittingly funny and their insights profound.

'And how is Egypt?' I asked heavily as I sat down, remembering that it was hot, dusty, smelly and full of interesting antiquities.

Lili spoke for a while and confirmed this. I also knew it could not possibly now be as boring as she was making it sound and I was annoyed with her. She seemed guarded, careful, as though she feared committing some solecism. This was most unlike her and beyond my understanding.

'You liked it didn't you, Margaret?' I asked, growing very tired now. 'Syl said you liked the people.'

He had found this surprising, which was why he had mentioned it to me. The British soldiers had returned from the desert wars with tales of feelthy postcards and baksheesh and peculiar goings on in Port Said, but I don't think it was that which had influenced Syl and caused his perturbation. I think it was because it was unusual for the English to express a fondness for any foreigners at all, and he saw it as a sign of unexpected originality in Margaret: something he had not bargained for. I had tried to tell him once or twice that I thought her clever beneath her pet-mouse exterior, but he didn't want to hear me.

'It was very nice,' said Margaret at her most bland.

'I miss it,' said Lili. 'I miss the heat and the colour.'

'And the noise?' I enquired. 'I remember it being very noisy in the cities. Monica always complained about the traffic.'

'The cities can be noisy,' agreed Lili.

I fervently wished they'd go home.

*

They did go eventually, just as dusk was falling. There were plenty of sandwiches left, so I gave one to the dog and he was grateful. I seldom gave him bread or things that might make him fatter, for I had a fearful fantasy that his taut shiny skin might not be sufficiently flexible to contain him and that he would go off *bang* like a sausage in the pan. I had a similar meaningless fear that if I should fall again I would break into a million shards like a saucer. I used to wonder what Syl's reaction would be if he returned home from work to find dog spattered all over the sitting room. I would have tried to get down on my hands and knees to sweep him up with the dustpan and brush and I would have fallen and shattered into pieces – dry, friable pieces compared with the viscous remains of pug. I was quite aware that there was an element of aggression in this distressing image. In a remote part of my mind I believed that Syl demanded too much of me, expected too much. I drew perverse satisfaction from the imagined expression on my son's face as he came upon the scene and realised

27

that he had asked too much of me; that his well-meant gift of a dog had brought about his mother's demise, and that anyway he had forced me to live too long by his unnatural dependence; that I had survived past the time when I should make a normal corpse and had drily exploded as burned bones turn to splinters and ash. I hasten to repeat that this thought did lie in a *remote* part of my mind. I was not going insane.

I put away the tea things in their accustomed places and went to clear the crumbs from the tea table. Mrs Raffald, the charwoman I shared with Monica, would be in in the morning but I couldn't leave the crumbs and the cigarette ash until then. Some crumbs fell on the floor and I called the dog to snuffle them up. A few crumbs could do him no harm. I went back to the kitchen. The smell of Lili's cigarettes had drifted through the house reminding me, not that she had just been there, but of the last time I had seen her.

My mind had an increasing tendency to make these slightly wrong connections, as though reaching for one drawer I had pulled open another. The smell of stale tea in the sink took me back to the farmhouse where the kitchen had been like a cathedral with hanging hams and bundled herbs for icons and the smell of apples, porridge cooked overnight on the range and roasting meat for incense. My present kitchen was not small by contemporary standards but it would have fitted six times into my uncles' kitchen. We had not formed the usual picture of a farming family despite this kitchen. My aunts always took tea in the afternoon in a little sitting-room in the back of the house-place. The kitchen quarters were known as the down-house and were more the province of the farmhands and the servants. The aunts had all smoked cigarettes when it was considered

28

unladylike to do so, and the woman who worked in the dairy smoked a clay pipe. The shallow stone sink always smelled of tea leaves in spite of all the other uses to which it was put and – I was homesick after sixty years of absence.

I began to prepare dinner for Syl, concentrating closely on what I was doing, not because I thought it wrong to live in the past – I've already said I didn't think it wrong – but because of the dangers of the heavy pans and the hot water and the floor which could become splashed and slippery and because dog and I could trip over each other. Monica had once alarmed Syl by telling him that old people frequently suffered from food poisoning, and indeed inflicted it on others, because they had lost their sense of smell. My sense of smell was in fine fettle. I could smell Lili's scent behind the smoke, and the chrysanthemums in the sitting-room. I could smell blood on the meat as I brought it from the pantry. So could the dog. *Go away dog.*

I cut up the meat carefully, for cold steel can be dangerous in trembling hands, and looked back a few weeks to the time Monica and Margaret had come to supper. I sliced carrots and chopped onions and tried, for safety's sake, to live in the present. Syl had bought a rack to keep the vegetables in. Before I knew it I was feeling the chill of a stone-flagged floor under my feet and peering into huge stone crocks for root vegetables of a similar size to bake together over the range coals. I could no more forget the farmhouse than ignore my own outworn body.

Monica and Margaret, I reminded myself, had come to supper on the day that we normally had stew, because the butcher called the day before and I always used up the stewing meat first. Joints for roasting could hang longer but I mistrusted the keeping properties of stewing steak. How boring it was to live in the present, I thought; how banal the minutiae of everyday existence. How much more delightful to revisit the scenes where such details had ceased to matter, where I could see firelight reflected in the windows and not fear the flames, smell wood smoke and cigarette smoke, hear the laughter of someone I loved because someone else I loved had just said something funny and not remember the joke, smell onions frying and not have to worry about the washing-up. There was no danger and no inconvenience in the past. I supposed that not all of it could be held blameless since it had brought me to what I was now, but it would be as futile to repine as to regret the ocean's flow.

If I had been a more religious woman I would probably have been considering life after death, but I could only think of what had gone before. If I had any hopes for the future they were that the past should be restored to me.

I had floured the meat and put it on the stove to brown. It was beginning to catch. I stirred it with a wooden spoon I had had all my life. One of the aunts had given it to me for Christmas long ago with a pudding bowl and a checked apron. The following Christmas my needs, my tastes and desires had changed and she had given me a beaded evening bag. That I had long since lost, but I still had the bowl and spoon of the last Christmas of my childhood. I had to go to the dining-room to see if there was a half-empty bottle of claret. There were plenty of full ones but I couldn't open them; nor was I sure which were sufficiently undrinkable to be used in cooking. Syl had a friend who was a wine merchant and sold him crates at a time. Some of it was at least not poisonous, but some of it, I was convinced, was so awful that it could only be palmed off on a friend whose concern for the relationship would prevent him from pouring it over the merchant's head.

Monica and Margaret had been subjected to a bottle of this because Syl – quite sincerely – took his father's view that women had no palate and good wine was wasted on them. I had argued with him about it, pointing out that I was a woman and I would prefer to drink the gardener's bath water, but Syl wouldn't listen. It was one of the things he had made up his mind about.

It had been an unenjoyable evening. The only person who had had a good time was Syl. He had his father's taste for company, and while he did not drink as Jack had done – indeed a very little alcohol went a long way with Syl – he liked the whole business of opening bottles and pouring liquid into glasses. We had gathered in the drawing-room and he had been the only creature present who showed any animation. The dog and I were tired as we always were in the evening; Margaret was as usual, and Monica was preoccupied. I had served supper with the minimum of fuss and formality and made no attempt to talk to Monica.

*

Monica had only once ever surprised me – some years ago now. One evening there had been a knock at the door. There was a summer storm going on, no rain yet but distant thunder, and lightning tearing up the night as though it were paper. It was so bright it shone through closed curtains, closed eyelids. It was late for visitors so, as Syl was in, I asked him to go and see who it was – not because I was nervous but I liked to remain on good terms with the neighbours and it was preferable for Syl to tell them that I was not in, rather than for me to appear unwelcoming.

I was in the kitchen mixing cocoa, quite a distance from the hall, but I could hear a woman talking. Oh God, it's some girl making trouble for Syl, I thought, and my skin felt odd with the apprehension you only feel for the people you love, a worse sensation than physical fear.

I went as silently as I could to the open kitchen door and listened. I could hear the woman weeping and then Syl said, 'Come and sit down, I'll get Mum.'

I was puzzled but reassured, for had it been one of his girls he would have tried to take her out of the house and soothe her down in the garden among the bushes so as not to upset me. It had happened before.

I went back to the stove to turn off the gas before the milk boiled over and waited for Syl to come and get me.

He said, 'It's Monica, Mum. I don't know what's wrong with her. Come and see, will you?'

I poured the milk into two mugs so that I could put the pan into cold water before it congealed, and I went to the sitting-room. She was sitting down but she got up as soon as she saw me.

I said, 'What on earth is it, Monica?' for she looked terrible.

She didn't even look like Monica. She was in her night-dress and resembled an elemental female creature from one of the more dispiriting myths – a harpy, a fury, a witch, somebody given to consuming the flesh of men. Her hair stood up all over the place, her face was wet with tears, scarlet and twisted with what I recognised as rage, and she was flexing her hands as though she was rending a living creature apart.

I said very sharply, 'Stop it, Monica. You look as though you're plucking a chicken.'

She laughed and I saw I had struck a wrong note, for these were days when women knew how to have hysterics. They had watched an older generation doing it and still found it a useful means of expression. The frustration of being forced into a role and told to keep quiet had caused many eruptions of shrieking hysteria in women when I was a girl. I had never needed recourse to it myself since I had refused the roles I was expected to assume and had always spoken my mind. Monica was normally so perfect an example of the English lady that this frenzy now seemed almost inevitable to me. I hoped I would not have to slap her face or dash cold water into it – two more *clichés* of the hysterical matrix.

I said again, 'What is it, Monica? Tell me at once and please sit down.'

When I had left college several people had suggested I should take up teaching, merely I think because I could so easily appear formidable. Even when I was a girl and not at all leading the sort of private life considered suitable to teachers I could put the fear of God into those around me by using a certain tone of voice. It was just another personal characteristic, of no more real significance than the shape of my nose, but it had often stood me in good stead.

Monica seemed to grow quieter and sat further into the chair instead of perching on the edge of it, poised to fly and sink her teeth in someone.

She said, 'Derek's leaving me.'

Her face contorted again as she made this announcement and I said, 'Syl, go and get the cocoa and give Monica a glass of brandy.'

He went gladly, never having enjoyed scenes.

I now noticed that some of the redness of her face was

due to a slap. I could see fingermarks. Clearly somebody else had been forced to apply the remedy for hysteria.

I said, startled, 'Did he hit you?'

Monica laughed again. 'I tried to kill him,' she said simply. 'He had to defend himself.'

This was by far the most interesting thing I had ever heard Monica say. I had never before seen so much as a crease in her conformity and this remarkable revelation put her in a different light.

'Where's Margaret?' I asked. I imagined that anxiety for her child would be uppermost in her mind after this scene of family violence, but it didn't seem to be.

'She's in bed,' she said.

'And where's Derek?' I enquired.

Monica was growing weary. 'He went out,' she said. 'I don't know where he went.'

I got up and called to Syl. 'Come and stay with Monica. I won't be a minute.'

He came reluctantly, bearing the cocoa, and poured out two glasses of brandy. As I went out I heard him beginning to talk about a committee meeting of the tennis club. It was probably the best way.

I went along the footpath that bordered the golf course and pushed through the gap in the hedge in Monica's garden. There was a light in the kitchen window and the back door was unlocked.

I called softly, 'Derek', in case he had come back, but there was no answer.

The house felt empty. The hall light was on too, illumining the way up the stairs.

I went very quietly to the nursery and opened the door. A night light glimmered on the chest of drawers and the child stood by the window looking out at the lightning over the rose-garden.

I was not what is known as 'good with children'. I had been well over forty when Syl was born. I couldn't remember how I had behaved towards him when he was very young and I couldn't remember ever dealing with other children. I had left all that to a succession of nannies.

I couldn't now remember how nannies behaved towards their charges; certainly no form of words came to me. Formality had been invented to ease those situations in which human beings find they have little in common and less to say to each other, so I said 'How are you, Margaret?' in a tone of great politeness.

She answered in her clear little voice, 'I'm very well, thank you.'

She showed no surprise at seeing me in her room, and no sign of fear. I wondered if she might be in shock and tentatively touched her hand. It was cold, but then so was the room; the window open top and bottom, the curtains drifting at their moorings in the night wind. I was silent and so was she. How could I ask whether she had overheard her mother trying to kill her father and whether she had minded very greatly?

She turned her head slightly to look at me but, it seemed, not in appeal – more as a well-bred adult might gaze at a stranger who had stayed too long and seemed to have no further purpose in remaining.

I said, 'Why don't you jump back into bed, Margaret?'

She obeyed at once and lay on her back, quite still. She was very small, her body scarcely perceptible under the bedclothes and I thought that in the circumstances I should take her in my arms and reassure her, but it would have appeared presumptuous. She was so self-possessed and undemanding.

I said, 'I'm going downstairs to wait for Mummy. I

35

won't go away.' I wanted to tell her some comforting lie
– 'Mummy came round to borrow a cup of sugar but we
couldn't find any so she's still looking', or 'Mummy and
I got bored with our own houses so we decided to
change places for the evening'. There was no suitable
lie, no explanation, and the truth seemed wholly
inappropriate for that quiet child.

There was a book lying on the table beside her bed
and I picked it up. It was full of brightly coloured
pictures of birds and I turned over the pages. 'Oh, look
at the robin, Margaret,' I said, feeling an awful fool.
'And here's a duck with its babies.'

To my surprise she sat up a little and leaned over to
look at this tiresome duck.

Encouraged, I flicked through the illustrations of tits,
starlings, wagtails until I came to a picture of a
kingfisher, and suddenly faced with that vivid,
unearthly green blue I was back in the country by a
deep tree-shaded river pool and there was a kingfisher
lying, startling in death, on the shoaly brink; one small,
flat space just large enough to contain it. I spoke
without thinking, or spoke my thoughts aloud: 'I found
a dead kingfisher once.'

She stared at me unblinkingly and said, 'It couldn't
fly.'

'No,' I agreed, feeling more than foolish now.

She had leaned further over to look more closely at
the picture and then settled back on her pillows.

As I went downstairs feeling remarkably useless, I
realised that she must have heard something or she
wouldn't be lying awake. It was too late now to do
anything about it. Whatever damage there was had
already been done to her.

After a while, as neither Monica nor Derek returned,

I telephoned Syl to ask what was going on. He spoke softly but without whispering, so I gathered that Monica had not left the house but Syl had closed the sitting-room door before answering the phone.

'She's sunk half the decanter of brandy,' he said.

'Has she told you what happened?' I asked.

Syl hesitated. 'She's told me some of it but I think there's more. She keeps opening her mouth and staring at me in a maddish kind of way, then closing it again...'

I interrupted him. 'Did she tell you she tried to murder Derek?'

'Well, she didn't quite put it like that...' said Syl.

I interrupted him again. 'Do you think she did?' I asked, suddenly wondering if a corpse was lying somewhere in this silent house.

'Oh come on, Mum,' said Syl. 'Monica's just upset...'

'How do you know?' I demanded, thinking of Monica's usual lady-like demeanour and the stories I had read of mild-mannered little men who the neighbours insisted wouldn't have hurt a fly and under whose cellar floors were found grisly things.

'I think what's really annoying her,' said Syl, now lowering his voice further, 'is that Derek's taken up with some teenaged typist.'

'Did he tell her?' I asked, reflecting that it was often this type of admission that led to murder.

'I think it was his parting shot,' said Syl. 'They were arguing about something or other and then he mentioned this girl – hang on...Monica, I'm just talking to Mum...'

'Hullo,' said Monica's voice still sounding high and strange as she took the phone. 'Has he come back?'

'No...' I said, intending to tell her that Margaret was all right.

But she wasn't listening. She said, 'Can I stay here? I don't want to see him.'

'Well, of course...' I said, but she'd hung up.

I sat all night wrapped in a rug I found in the cloakroom. I'd locked the doors and I must admit I took a cursory survey of the ground floor to ascertain that Derek's lifeless body was not indeed littering up some corner. Then I stayed awake reading one of Monica's novels in case Margaret should cry out. I thought it strange that Monica had not mentioned the child. She was usually an oppressively careful mother.

That one display of emotion had been as shocking and strange as if she'd suddenly taken all her clothes off. She had kept out of my way for months afterwards and I hadn't sought her out. Derek had returned, for I saw him several times and found it difficult to think of much to say to him. Eventually he left for good. I had no idea how the divorce went through, but Monica and the child stayed in the house and gradually we began to see her again – at the tennis club and in neighbours' houses. She never mentioned that naked night, and I certainly did not. There is fortunately a mechanism in us which works like the gates of a lock, interrupting and blocking the flow of memory, of immediate awareness. Once the gates are closed, although we know the water is there and it is still the same, we can disregard it, think of it as past and, often, forget it. This, I suppose, is what Monica did: put out of her mind the bad things drifting and floating behind the gates, and drove resolutely onwards, refusing even to acknowledge their existence.

*

Syl was late getting home. I heard him whistling in the

hall and called out to him.

'Not in bed yet?' he said.

'No,' I said. When you have lived with someone for a long time, no matter who he is, this seems to be the sort of conversation you make. I asked if he had had a pleasant day and he said he had. Then, since it was his turn, he asked if I had had a pleasant tea with Margaret and Lili.

'Very nice,' I said. 'There's some cake in the pantry. Or do you want some soup?'

'I've eaten,' said Syl. 'Went to the pub in the city.'

'Who with?' I asked.

'Just a bloke,' said Syl. He looked at me sideways and grinned.

'Bloke?' I said. 'What was he like?' Syl seldom whistled when he came home after dining with a bloke.

'He was a nice little blonde from the office,' said Syl.

'You're nearly a married man,' I said. 'It's time you settled down.'

'I'm going to, Mum,' said Syl. 'Honestly.'

I believed him: perhaps not because I trusted his intentions but because he sometimes looked so tired. I could see that settling down would come as a relief. Married men did not have to prove themselves capable of attracting women – not, that is, until they grew rather older than Syl and in need of a further dose of reassurance. That had been Jack's trouble. When he was really quite old he had begun to strut in the presence of women. He had always fancied himself as a bit of a lad, as they say, but he grew silly, especially when there were younger men present. He could not resist the temptation of cutting out younger men, even if it was only by hogging the conversation. He was entirely predictable, and after a while I didn't go out with him if

39

I could help it. It was boring. Besides I had enough residual fondness for him not to enjoy watching him make an idiot of himself. I could not, naturally, remonstrate with him because that would have been construed as jealousy and have led to long passages of misunderstanding. I don't suppose there's a man in the world who would believe you had only his interests at heart if you asked him not to flirt with other women. I had sometimes wished he would take a mistress, particularly after he retired and was at home more. Luckily the golf course was just behind the house and he spent a lot of time there, but it wasn't the same as when he had to spend weeks away and I knew I had the place to myself – and Syl of course.

I have often noticed that when a man takes a mistress it greatly improves his demeanour in the marital home. Whether this is because of guilt or satisfied desire I do not know, but I have always remarked it. It is important for the wife that the mistress should be a serious, responsible sort of person, and luckily they frequently are. Men tire quite soon of the dizzy gold-digger of legend, and a surprising number of 'other women' are more homely and steady than many wives. These excellent creatures help to ease the pressure put on a couple by the exigencies of married life; they uphold the man's self-esteem so that he does not need to wear himself out demonstrating his virility, and they enable the wife – if she is capable and prepared to do so – to uncover an identity of her own, to escape, to some degree at least, the stifling confines of wifehood. Jack unfortunately had not enough self-confidence to take a permanent mistress but contented himself with ogling girls. I was painfully ashamed of (and for) him, but I could think of no formula by which I could make him understand his error. I think he believed that if his liaisons were brief, shallow and impersonal no harm could come of them. He was unaware that his loss of dignity which should have, and did not, trouble him caused me sleepless nights. I could have borne the compassion (not infrequently mixed with respect) which is accorded to the wife whose husband has another *ménage*, but not the pity, the mirth, to which a husband's ceaseless, pointless, trivial dalliance exposes a wife. How does one explain such things to a man?

Perhaps now I can bring myself to speak of Lili and why I had hoped never to have to see her again. She must have been in her early twenties when it happened, when Jack was nearly fifty. He was at the height of his flirtatious career and a trial to me. Whenever we were invited out together I would make some excuse and stay at home reading, so that already people found me distant, cold and unfriendly. In a way that has been a blessing. Having established quite early that I was not a gregarious woman I have been largely left alone. I never could abide drunken conviviality, and when my *ennui* was compounded by the awareness that I had chosen to marry a foolish and insecure man I vowed never more to go out in society. Jack would say – his body freshly bathed and powdered and his face pink from shaving – 'Come on, darling. Come too. You'll enjoy it. You know you like the so-and-sos.' And I would say, 'No, my dear. You go alone. I am determined to finish *Swann's Way* by the end of the month.' The mention of Proust always alarmed him. He would say, 'Well, if you're sure...' and off he would go, tremulous and excited as a child. (He was very like Syl. My poor Syl...)

But I was speaking of Lili: my mind wanders. It must

41

have been a few days after the picnic in the garden. Monica and Derek had just returned from Egypt and Monica was giving a cocktail party as a farewell gesture to Lili and Robert who were about to go back again, and I had pleaded a headache. 'Too much sun,' I think I said: I would have an early night and perhaps come round in the morning to help her clear up and also finish the unpacking. I was about to go to bed when the telephone rang. Monica was in a housewifely state because she couldn't find the crate with the extra glasses. Would I lend her some? She'd send a couple of people round to collect them.

I said she wasn't to bother. If she sent Derek he would feel obliged to insist that I return with him to the party. It wouldn't be seemly to borrow my wine glasses and then leave me in peace. It wouldn't be correct. I said I would put some in a cardboard box and bring them round.

I set off along the path by the golf course, walking very carefully because the glasses were loosely assembled and the bottom of the box was likely to drop open. When I reached the summer-house I rested the box on the narrow window-ledge in order to readjust my grip. Then, unthinkingly, I looked through the window. My body darkening the window must have given them warning of my presence, for Jack was already staring out at me, his face stiff with dismay, a parody: 'We are discovered. All is undone...' Lili didn't look at me. I think she was too busy smoothing down her dress. I went on to the house, cold with rage. Not because Jack had been unfaithful to me again, but because Lili knew I knew, and would be harbouring feelings that I should find unacceptable: possibly guilt, but I already knew her well enough to doubt that: pity

42

for me – perhaps compunction – since she was not really a heartless girl. I thought she would not be feeling triumphant, for she was too clever to misunderstand my attitude to Jack.

I had banged down the glasses in the kitchen and realised that what was so infuriating was that she probably knew exactly what I was thinking: knew I didn't love him, knew I didn't care what he did, knew I cared a good deal that I was married to a fool, knew that I knew she knew what she did know. She might even know that somewhere in me was pity for Jack: the coiled contemptuous pity for somebody who, thinking that he is exhibiting his manhood, has merely been caught with his trousers down. I suffered an insupportable, vicarious sense of degradation. When my mother had run away with another man and left me and my father, I had felt bitter hurt but not this extended humiliation. A woman can never seem as ridiculous as a man, since whatever pride she may have is more broadly based and therefore less vulnerable. Her transgressions may arouse great passion, even scorn, but seldom that profound, half-hysterical contempt. Lili had lost no dignity since she had never laid claim to it.

Someone said, 'You must have a drink now you're here.' But as I had come in the guise of a messenger, a porter, and not really as a guest, his words were not pressing and I was allowed to leave.

Soon after, Lili left the country and I thought never to see her again. My sudden appearance had caused Jack such fright and shock that he became what he considered to be a model husband – that is, he hardly went anywhere at all unless I could be prevailed upon to go with him and he frequently stayed in of an evening. He said he didn't know what had come over him and it would never happen again. I could think of nothing to say, but I used to wish that I could get my hands on Lili. I forgot about her, but I never forgave her.

Shortly afterwards Jack died. Sometimes I wished that he could have died before his pride was lost, and sometimes I didn't care. I haven't really cared about anything since – except Syl.

*

In one way I was relieved that Syl had not married until now. My family had been Catholic since Adam was a lad. They had lived in a remote corner of the North and the upheavals of the 'reformation' had not troubled them. None of us had been called to martyrdom and we all took the Faith for granted, like air and bread. When my mother left my father all those years ago, the gentry and the yeomanry for miles around had been delightfully scandalised, for adultery and divorce were social sins and rare in those parts. But my uncles and aunts, her kin, without talking, or even thinking, about it, feared for her immortal soul. They were ashamed in the social sense and angry with her for so shaming them, but those emotions are bearable. It is the knowledge that somebody you love – one of you – might, by sin, separate herself from you for eternity that is a source of anguish. Embarrassment and wrath kept my family away from the neighbours for a time, but it was not those feelings which would make one of my uncles fall silent, another give a sudden exclamation and bite his lip. It was not because my mother had put her sisters into the awkward position of having to hold their heads high before the curious regard of the neighbours, when what they wanted was to clap their hands over their

44

ears, close their eyes and pretend they were insensate that made one of my aunts weep silently in church and another take to saying Decades of the Rosary at peculiar moments. It was the fear that one of them was lost.

Perhaps it was the fear that marriage presented a choice between temporal misery or eternal hell that kept me single for so long. I had plenty of offers and fell in love a few times, but I felt no inclination to tie myself up. When I really did fall in love I expected and asked too much. I should have known better. I had seen enough of my friends making similar mistakes and given them excellent advice on strategy, on anodyne devices and curative measures. I remembered none of them. When the only man I ever loved finally left me, I married Jack. I had forgotten my dread of marriage when I found a man I couldn't bear to lose, and when I lost him I found I had lost everything – even that lifelong dread. I was nearly forty by then and so had less life to throw away. I liked Jack, and he loved me. He was a little younger than I was but I didn't exploit this. I had learned not to appear too dominating and I left all the major decisions to him. He didn't do badly, and I was fairly content. It wasn't the life I would have chosen but it was comfortable and it had its compensations. We spent most of the time abroad even after Syl was born until we moved here.

Where was I? I was saying that, in the main, I was quite glad that Syl hadn't married until now. He would have, as I had had, less time to rue the day. I wished now that I had brought him up differently and not left him so much in the care of the nannies and schools. He had too fixed a view of what constituted masculinity. He was afraid of showing weakness, and felt called upon to flirt with every female who crossed his path, regardless

45

of whether or not she appreciated his attention. Whether or not he was consciously emulating his father, it was a great pity. I could see that some people found it hard to take him seriously. Jack had always strenuously maintained that there were some things men did and some things for women to do. I was perfectly competent in practical matters, but Jack – who was less competent than I – took all such things upon himself and my skills atrophied. I don't know now that I would remember how to put a washer on a tap. Not that it matters any more. It just seems unfortunate that the sexes should limit each other in this rigid fashion. I had always found satisfaction in being self-sufficient. The idea that two separate beings should restrict themselves to certain roles in order to form one whole seemed to me to be structurally unsound. There was a makeshift ring to it. When the string breaks, as it so frequently does, the wear and tear of the operation will have damaged even further the two parts of the unnatural whole. I had discussed this question with priests I had known, and various religious, and been soundly reprimanded for my thoughts, which they considered, to say the least, unorthodox. I had been bred to respect the priesthood and so never said precisely what I felt – that it was all very fine and large for them, speaking from their superior position of celibacy: it was we, poor foot soldiers, who had to slog through the mire of matrimony. Despite our staunch adherence to the Faith our family had not been much blessed with vocations. I was not a good Catholic, but I could not have married somebody who wasn't one at all, and I would have been greatly perturbed if Syl had done so. Margaret, in that respect, came as a relief to me.

Margaret? No, I couldn't really understand her. I

have said she was like me and, having said it, cannot remember the reason. Undemanding, unobtrusive: I am that now but I wasn't when I was Margaret's age. Those of us with any health in us at all change as we grow and I wondered how Margaret would change, or whether she would stay as she was and simply, in the course of time, wither. Either way, as I considered it, it did not augur well for Syl's peace of mind or his contentment. Then I told myself I was guilty of that male fault of over-analysis, of pointless prognostication, and turned, as it were, to look on the bright side again. The old are too prone to misgivings. It was true that Syl was over-protective towards her, over-indulgent, and sometimes over-attentive – although not always. Once he took her away for the weekend to stay with a man he'd been at school with. The man had an adopted son, who was about Margaret's age and very full of himself. I told Syl I did not think this weekend a good idea and he stared at me in wonder and asked why. I said feebly that if past form was anything to go by he and his friend would spend the time together engaged in manly pursuits and Margaret would be bored. What I really feared was that youth, as they say, would call to youth, and Margaret would come to her senses in the presence of the lad who was, as I remembered, a lively, attractive boy despite his conceit. 'She'll have the kid to talk to,' Syl had said. 'He's going through an anti-blood-sports phase, and sits around indoors all day.' I couldn't think of anything to say. How do you explain to a man that you fear a younger man will cut him out by being lazy and gentle in what could be construed as a feminine fashion, while he himself is ploughing across the countryside proving his masculinity. There is no meeting-ground here. I have never met a man who could see that wit and a kind of reticence – which could almost be called cowardice – make up a combination which, in some men, and perhaps in some women too, is virtually irresistible. Physical prowess has in it an element of boastfulness – 'Watch me' – which inevitably, albeit unjustly, gives its owner a certain appearance of bone-headedness. The sly smile of the aesthete has got more people into bed than the triumphant grin of the long-distance runner. I know. I wondered hopelessly why, after all this time, men didn't know that as well. I see that I have said I feared that Margaret might 'come to her senses', and have exposed my reservations. Another girl of her age might not have been too unsuitable for Syl, but she was.

I put these unpleasant thoughts aside, as is the way of human kind. Increasing age does not increase one's acceptance of anything, not even death.

'Did you have a good time?' I had asked Syl when I saw him at breakfast on the Monday morning.

'Splendid,' said Syl. 'I put a brace of pheasants in the larder.'

'Did Margaret enjoy herself?' I asked.

Syl was eating a boiled egg and looked for a second as though he'd forgotten who she was. 'Oh yes,' he said, through a mouthful of toast, 'she had a splendid time.'

I sipped lukewarm tea while I waited for him to go to work. He'd promised to pluck the pheasants so I hung them even further out of the reach of the dog who had sneaked into the larder and was looking up at them like a poet at the stars. How ridiculous that I should remember that so well.

*

Lili had left a cigarette packet on the window-seat. I found it in the morning as I sat drinking tea and watching the birds. There were two cigarettes in it and on a whim I went and got a match from the kitchen, came back, sat down and lit one.

It was years since I'd given up smoking. I had stopped when I was expecting my first child – not for reasons of health or morality, but because it made me sick. The child, a girl, had died in infancy and when they told me she was dead I had said, 'Give me a cigarette.'

Infancy: the word is like a little diaphanous shroud to cover up the unbearable. She had been five days old. They came to me and they said, 'Mrs Carter...' (I had assumed the name. This was before I had married Jack. The child was illegitimate.) They said: 'The child was too small to live. She never really had a chance...' I drew on my cigarette and said: 'Surely she was a little young to die.' The doctor held my shoulder briefly, and then left without saying anything. The nurse fussed about for a while doing what nurses do, not saying anything either. I think she was humming a little tune under her breath. They were both afraid of me, but they need not have been. I lay and looked at the ceiling and smoked and promised myself that nothing should ever hurt like this again. I didn't cry or rant or do anything much except arrange for the baby to be properly buried in her own baby grave. There were just the priest and me there on a watery spring morning, and all I can remember feeling was disbelief and a desperate yearning for it to end, so that I could smoke. It was soon over. I sat on a gravestone and smoked and smoked, my hand shielding the cigarette until it was possible no longer with the rain pouring down my face.

Then when I was pregnant with Syl I had stopped

smoking again. I dreaded the birth of this child. I had not before felt such grief, such pity for the as yet unborn. It was like the grief one feels for the dead. It was worse, for even if there is no God and no abode to share with him, at least the dead are past all pain, while those who are yet to be born must learn to live with us: with our frailty and our cruelty. They must learn in time, in order to survive, to be like us. When Syl was very young I was afraid – more of, than for, him – terrified of the beloved's capacity for pain; and as he grew older I indulged him, trying to protect him from his human heritage. A mistake.

Memories are like possessions: furniture, ornaments. Some are always in the room of your mind, some decayed, some lost; and some are there on the walls – of no further profit or use and never to be shared or revealed. Only you yourself are aware that the small hidden image gleaming barely perceptibly through the dust represents the hinge and focus of your life. You tell yourself it doesn't matter and God alone knows what you think you mean.

I don't know why I said all that. I have never spoken of it to anyone. It was the taste of cigarette smoke that brought it back – more potent than any little biscuit, than any egg sandwich. I never did finish the whole of Proust. There wasn't any point after Jack died. Once I was alone I had no need of feints and ruses and avenues of escape since I could be solitary in truth and fact, not just in metaphor. Poor Jack. He was, while a stupider, also a better person than me, in the sense that he was more truly human. I had a capacity for, and knowledge of, evil, while Jack's misdemeanours seemed somehow on a par with the failings of the dog. Having said that, I do not think I could construct a worse insult if I tried

50

from now until the end of time, and I am glad that Jack is dead and beyond harm for I might once have been angry enough to tell him so. Presumably the offensiveness lies in the nature of evil, and now I am confused. It does not seem to me that I think less clearly than I did, but I get tired more easily and I lose the thread. I was thinking of humanity as a combination of beast and angel. It is the beasts who are sinless and it was the brightest angel in Heaven who turned his face from the light. It is the angel in us who is capable of sin; the poor beast merely seeks gratification. I feel I should apologise to Jack, and then I feel – what the hell, this is nothing but the truth. Except, of course, that it isn't and humanity is yet another order of being, more complex than we can ever know.

*

I finished the cigarette just as Mrs Raffald arrived. She looked at me with exaggerated surprise, and I stubbed it out in a saucer.

'You look as if you'd been doing that all your life,' she said.

'It isn't difficult,' I told her.

'*You're* not a smoker,' she said, unbuttoning her coat and taking her hat off.

'I used to be,' I said. 'I used to smoke as much as Lili.'

Mrs Raffald paused on her way to the broom-cupboard. '*She* smokes too much,' she remarked. 'You can smell her coming a mile off.'

Mrs Raffald and I enjoyed a cordial, even close, relationship. We understood each other.

'My aunts all smoked until they died in their nineties,' I said, remembering them. Elegant in age, smoke

51

furling in the lamplight, they had talked and talked in the swift, clipped tones of their generation that would seem artificial now. It was strange to think of those days and their difference. There had been more noise, more bustle: even, it seemed, more light. But that was because there had been fewer lights – no electricity in the farm, gas-lighting in the streets – and so the light had had more significance, had shone more brightly. The street lamps in the road now cast a bland glow half prudish, half prurient. They said, 'Nothing unseemly can go on under our regard, and if it does we will be watching.' I remembered a time when I had walked home to the farm from the village because I had somehow missed the uncle sent to collect me. I had been to a music lesson and I hummed 'Farewell Manchester' until I reached the edge of the houses. It was pitch black beyond. I felt my way along the hedgerow, knowing that I must not stop and turn, for if I did I should have no idea which direction I was headed in. When I came to the moor I half walked, half crawled until I saw the lights of the farmhouse. It was both frightening and not frightening. There had been no marauders or footpads in the district since the previous century, but as I edged through that utter darkness I felt I would welcome the company of any other living thing – a wild animal, a murderer. Only when I saw the lights of home did normal apprehension return and the hairs on my neck rise as I heard a rustle in the marsh grass, breathing behind a low stone wall. When home is within reach, sheep become tigers and the swooping owl the assassin. I think it is hope which makes us cowards.

'Well, don't take it up again,' advised Mrs Raffald, returning equipped with broom and dustpan and brush. 'Not at your age.'

'No,' I said absently, for I was wondering why in total darkness there is nothing to fear but darkness. Then I thought about what she had said. 'If you think about it,' I observed, 'this is the only sensible age to do anything dangerous.'

'Oh you,' said Mrs Raffald. 'Philosopher, you are. You should see what's going on down at The Oaks. Three-ring circus down there. Telephone calls, and wedding dresses, and Lili leaving her stuff all over the place.'

I found it interesting but not surprising that Mrs Raffald should refer to Lili by her Christian name. She would not in a million years have done the same by Monica. 'Weddings are always a nuisance,' I said.

'I prefer a funeral,' said Mrs Raffald. 'Unless it's somebody close,' she added. 'The food's generally better.'

'I suppose that's true,' I said, 'and they don't hand you fizzy drinks. Champagne gives me indigestion these days, and I hate those little nibbles that fill you up but don't stop you feeling hungry.'

'Yes,' said Mrs Raffald with the brevity of the connoisseur. Her own family and friends were always getting married, being christened or dying, and she was also frequently called upon to help when my neighbours found themselves in the midst of these traumatic events.

'Is the dress finished yet?' I asked. Monica had been extremely boring about the dress.

'Dunno,' said Mrs Raffald, sweeping the ashes from the grate. 'Margaret moons about all day like a dying duck in a thunderstorm. S'pose she must be in love.'

She said this with such an airy lack of conviction that I was taken aback. I had somehow assumed that Margaret must be in love with Syl, and thought no more about it.

53

Plenty of women had been. Why not Margaret? But now I remembered other things I had once taken for granted: the illness of one of my uncles which had killed him before we could, any of us, accept even that he was ailing. Nothing could have saved him, but we should have been better prepared.

'Have you seen her in it?' I asked.

'In what?' said Mrs Raffald, dusting the iron bars.

'The dress,' I said patiently, perhaps thinking that if I could hear how she wore her wedding dress I would know how she felt about her wedding.

'No,' said Mrs Raffald. 'Her mum just goes on about it all the time. Dress this, dress that. Too long, too short. Don't know why she doesn't just chuck it out and get a new one.'

'She wore it at her own wedding,' I reminded Mrs Raffald. 'Didn't she tell you?'

'Oh yes,' said Mrs Raffald. 'She told me all right. You'd think she'd want to forget about it, being divorced all this time – not make the poor kid wear it.'

I reflected that Monica would die on the spot if she could hear us: the mother of the groom discussing the bride's family with the charwoman.

'Monica doesn't think a great deal,' I said, out of an obscure sense of vengefulness. I had too often been bored or irritated by her.

'Oh, she's all right really,' said Mrs Raffald generously. 'She just got a bit spoilt having all those servants out East. There's quite a few like that round here.'

It was true. There were, and Monica was far from the worst amongst them. Mrs Trevelyan from The Cedars, for instance, was a poisonous bitch with an entirely tenuous grasp of current reality. No, Monica was not too bad.

54

'The Colonial experience,' I said aloud, 'had a bad effect on the English underbred.'

Mrs Raffald agreed. She said she didn't know how the poor natives had taken it, but when people like Mrs Trevelyan came back and tried it on with her she soon let them know where they got off.

When she'd finished sweeping the drawing-room I made us both a cup of coffee and I thought about the woman who had worked in my uncles' dairy and had smoked a pipe. She was called Marge, and she called all of us, even the eldest uncle, by our Christian names. I had had maids since then, and native servants when Jack did a stint in Egypt, and they had all made me uneasy. Northern blood does not adapt easily to an atmosphere of voluptuousness, of servility and craft – and all these things are present, in no matter how small a degree, in the type of master-servant relationship which Mrs Raffald and I were presently engaged in denigrating.

'Lili's all right,' said Mrs Raffald as she drank her coffee. 'She shows off a bit, but not so's anyone would mind.'

I couldn't dispute this. I was no longer angry with Lili. Jack was dead.

*

I sometimes found it strange to realise how little effect the vast cataclysms of existence have on those of us who are not too directly inconvenienced by them. The war for instance. Jack had been too old for active service and was given a job in one of the Ministries, which kept him employed and out of the way and allowed him the additional excitement of fire-watching from the roof when the bombing was at its height; while Syl was unfit. It transpired at his medical examination that his heart was weakened, probably by an undiagnosed attack of rheumatic fever when he was a child. That was possibly the worst fright I had throughout the war. Extraordinarily enough, I knew no one who had lost either a husband or a son and what I remember chiefly about those years is discomfort rather than fear or horror. We had the air-raid shelter dug in the garden, but when I was alone I never bothered to use it. Jack was away most nights – possibly fire-watching, probably not – and when the siren went I would settle in the blacked-out dining-room on a temporary divan bed with a book and a bottle and a supply of candles in case the electricity failed. I had an irrational feeling that I would prefer to sleep downstairs and let the house fall in on me than sleep in the bedroom and come down with the house. Syl was away most of the time working out ciphers and codes, I believe, at some secret place in the country. He never spoke about it. He was out of the front line and I hardly worried. I joined the WVS and I knitted socks for sailors, and I conceived the same hatred as the rest of my countrymen for the sign of the somersaulting child, the swastika. I dealt not at all with the Black Market, and very little 'under the counter', and I never breached the black-out rules or wasted a single crust of bread. When the war was over we filled in the air-raid shelter and built the rockery over it, and as the years went by the only time I thought about the war was when I realised that butter and cream were unrationed and I could swim in them if I liked. I am ashamed of this remoteness: not because, like some idiotic folk I have met, I feel guilty because I did not suffer, but because it seems that only suffering can impress events on our minds and consciousness and this makes us seem paltry.

Lili showed very little bitterness when she spoke of how her family's wealth had been taken away, and I admired her for this. I didn't lose this feeling of admiration even when I understood that, by various shifts and devices, much of her family had contrived to retain much of its riches. Things were not and never would be the same. She had an *insouciance* which I do not think I should have been capable of in her circumstances. There had been bred in my bones a respect, almost a love, for property which would have made it impossible for me to accept with so little complaint the appropriation of land which belonged to me. By property I mean only land. Other possessions left me cold. If, when I was a girl, the farmhouse had been forcibly taken from us I would have fought and killed to keep it. Now it no longer mattered. The course of life had separated me from my land and it was no longer mine. In truth it never had been. I had never held the deeds to it, after all, but it had belonged to me because I belonged to it. I had felt, like a peasant, that I needed it for sustenance and for identity; but I had drifted away, and now I was nobody but old Mrs Monro, living nowhere but in a meaningless house surrounded by spotted laurels. I told myself that it was probably intensely good for my soul: as was the reluctant esteem which I felt for Lili's seemingly spontaneous renunciation of what had been hers.

*

I still liked to do my own shopping. Most of the tradesmen called at the house, but sometimes I would find an excuse to go to the shops. I needed some exercise and I detested walking in Croydon unless I had an aim in view. I walked slowly, masochistically reminding myself of the times when I had run over the moors and down the lanes. *So long ago.* All I knew of history seemed fresher and more immediate than my own youth. Ann Bullen, poor girl, and Mary Queen of Scots, and Margaret of York who was pressed to death under slabstones for refusing to renegue on her faith – I could visualise them, soft-skinned and damp with fear as death faced them – but my own youthful self had disappeared into the past, not come with me to my present state. It was as though, at some point, I had been reinvented – an old woman to take the place of the young one. Did I envy those dead girls? Or had Margaret of York come into my head to remind me of *my* Margaret, and why did I think of her as mine when I did not, to be frank, really much care for her? And why was I walking to the butcher when my hips ached? Silly old woman.

I wished I had brought dog for company. But dog, after a very short while, would have had to be carried, and there were difficulties implicit in carrying both dog and a parcel of meat. I was very sad that day. No gleam showed through the fabric that separates us from eternity, and I felt mortal, carnal and disposed to decay. Perhaps it was merely because I was going to the butcher. He was brisk as ever behind his counter, wielding his cleaver, smiting through the bones and joints of dead animals and addressing his customers with his usual *bonhomie*. Butchers are more aggressively cheerful than any other tradesmen, and I wondered why. I had come across melancholy bakers, grim-faced and truculent grocers, and all female shop assistants seemed reluctant to be in that position, aggrieved and resentful at the necessity of having to serve the public, but butchers always appeared pleased with life, positive and willing in their attitude. I wished I knew some undertakers to see if proximity to death had the same effect on them – not, of course, when they were actively engaged in their trade, but when they were at home with their families or out with the boys.

I was relieved to meet Mrs Raffald outside the newsagents as I walked home with a pound of stewing steak and a sheep's heart for dog.

'What are you doing here?' she asked, with a kind of fond disapproval.

'Shopping,' I said humbly, pleased to have my thoughts interrupted.

'You should've asked *me*,' she said. 'If you'd wanted something I'd've got it for you.'

'I felt like a walk,' I said. 'I get stiff sitting at home all day.'

'You just missed Lili,' she said. 'The butcher says "Who's that tart staying up with them at The Oaks?" She smiled.

'She does give that impression – ' I began and stopped, for surely nothing demanded that I should dissemble to Mrs Raffald: not female nor class solidarity.

'She *is* a tart,' I agreed and ended lazily, 'but she's got a heart of gold.' Mrs Raffald would not scorn my *clichés*. She understood Lili, I was sure, as well as I did and no refinement of expression, no careful character analysis were needed from me in order to shelter Lili's worth in the eyes of my charwoman.

Mrs Raffald justified my assessment. 'I like her too,' she said.

She walked with me to the end of the street and I felt better. I forgot about undertakers, which was fortunate, for at my age it does not raise the spirits to dwell too closely on their *raison d'être*.

*

One Saturday I went for another walk. Not to the shops this time. I went along the path by the bottom of the gardens, taking dog as a treat. He waddled among the dead leaves looking, I suppose, for dead things to devour. I was thinking about something I had once said to a man who loved me, that we had grown too close and must be sundered, and wondering why I had said it. In truth I was again thinking about Margaret, for I sensed in her a revulsion from intimacy. I felt tired and I walked slowly.

As I came to the garden of The Oaks I caught a glimpse of Syl and Margaret standing very close together and I thought that I must have been mistaken about her. She must have loved Syl to permit him to stand so close to her. I walked on, feeling, not reassured, but confused.

As I turned to walk home again I saw Syl in front of me. Dog put on a spurt to catch up with him, wheezing awfully, his little legs seeming inadequate to his ambitions.

'Dog,' I called, 'wait for me.'

Syl stopped and looked round. He smiled when he saw me and I took his arm.

'Where's Margaret?' I asked.

'She went in,' said Syl. 'She was cold.'

He sounded perfectly relaxed and confident but I thought it odd: strange that a girl in love, with nothing to do that day, should go in because she was cold.

'Why didn't she get a coat?' I asked.

Syl laughed. 'Because there was no point. I couldn't stay. I've got a game this afternoon.'

Dog had disappeared. 'Where's dog?' I said. 'Dog, dog...' I raised my voice. He emerged suddenly from a shallow ditch, a dead leaf over one ear. 'Come here you little beast.' I picked him up, all muddy and wet as he was and carried him home.

I had made scones that morning. The smell of them still hung in the air and it broke my heart. It went with the smell of home, and this wasn't home. I had no home, Syl had no home, dog had no home. We just all lived together. I rubbed dog dry with no affection and no enthusiasm. Dead leaf over one ear or not, I no longer found him endearing. He was just an old dog somebody had given me once. Syl was somebody I had given birth to once and I could only feel sorrow for him. I poured myself a sherry and after a while I felt better.

'What are you doing?' asked Syl sharply as he looked in at the sitting-room before going off for his game.

'Drinking,' I said.

He stood looking at me for rather a long time without saying anything.

I took no notice. I knew I grew easily fuddled with drink these days. I could hear myself repeating myself. Myself, myself, I thought, sick of myself and my old bones. In the evenings after a few drinks I was no fit company for anyone.

'I don't care,' I said aloud, and Syl made no reply but went off to play his game.

*

Lili now began to call on me quite often. She would come in through the back door, calling 'Cuck-oo', stripping off her coat and dropping it at the foot of the stairs. And, do you know, I didn't mind. I began to half wait, half hope that she would come, smelling of scent and cigarettes and talking of things that other people didn't talk about. She never mentioned Jack, but after a while I found myself saying his name as I talked of the past. It would have been unnatural not to do so, like describing a recipe and leaving out a mundane but essential ingredient. Of course she had not forgotten the occasion when she had seduced my husband, but she didn't speak of it, although I would not have been entirely surprised if she had done so. As it was, whenever I said his name she would look straight into my eyes with a smiling, limpid regard and offer me a cigarette. As often as not I would accept it. I did not feel old when Lili was with me because she did not treat me with the strained respect which most people considered appropriate to the elderly. Men who habitually told risqué stories would moderate their language in my presence, rendering themselves even more tiresome, since constraint causes such unease. I used to toy with the idea of uttering some unspeakable word, but such words come as ill from withered lips as from the lips of babies. I don't know why this should be so. It is probable that the old have undergone more experiences which require such words to describe them than have the young. Perhaps we are meant to have forgotten them all, and, if I am to be honest, perhaps we have. I could not remember the passions that had once filled me – only the broken splinters of phrases that I had used to express them: '...don't leave me. I'll kill you/myself, I can't bear it.' Of the happier moments I could recall almost nothing, not even the words. This was really a mercy, for people who are in love are like people who are out of their minds, and it is best to forget what they say. Passion dies. Even love poetry has a faded scent to those who entomb dead desire, and everyday words by everyday people attempting to convey their emotions are possibly the most banal in the language. Lili, I was sure, was not at the moment in love. She was far too lively and interesting, discussing everything under the sun, not half-hypnotised by obsession or limp with wondering what the beloved was up to. She said one day, – à propos of nothing much – I don't know what I had said to lead her on:

'It's no use anyone asking me about relationships. When I was a little child I was sometimes spoiled, and sometimes locked in my room, and as a result I find it difficult to form relationships.'

'Who told you that?' I asked.

'I did,' said Lili. 'At one point I was being very bad about relationships and Robert said I should be psychoanalysed. That is very expensive and we were short of money, so I simply asked myself what this psychoanalyst would say. He would say "Lili", he would say to me, "as a child, Lili, it has become evident from what you have told me that you were sometimes spoiled and sometimes locked in your room. This has made it difficult for you to form relationships." Then he would say, "That will be ten guineas. You must come back tomorrow, and the next day, and the next, and the next until you can make perfect relationships" – like perfect omelettes – and we would have been penniless and that would have been worse than the bad relationships. Don't you agree?'

'What bad relationships?' I asked. 'You've been married for donkey's years.'

'I don't really have a relationship with Robert,'

explained Lili, 'so it can't be bad. But with other people – I tend to squeeze them like lemons until I have squeezed out all the juice, and then I fling them aside.'

'I see,' I said.

'Not women,' said Lili. 'I have good relationships with women. Only men.'

I said I saw very little value in paying out good money in order to have more mutually satisfactory affairs, and Lili said that of course I was right: that was what she had thought herself. She said she also thought that Robert was unlike a lemon, and more like a potato, in that he was not susceptible to squeezing.

Most people seek to be reassuring when health, whether bodily or mental, is under discussion, so I said that that was fortunate, that Robert's potato-like quality must represent strength, solidarity and endurance. Lili said nothing as I spoke and, since she did not deny what I was saying, after a while I fell to thinking – as I had sometimes thought before – that words could be used as the stuff of illusion: that, marshalled in a certain order so that they made at least grammatical sense, they could be used to silence the dissident, awe the credulous, inflame the mob to violence and almost always dazzle the unintelligent; that words were not like bones, a basic and necessary structure, but more like the inessential finery which people flaunt to gain a better conceit of themselves and impress their fellows.

I said, 'I talk too much. I suppose it's because I'm so often alone.'

'You don't talk too much,' said Lili.

'I sometimes talk a lot of nonsense,' I said, 'but then so do we all.'

'I rather like it,' said Lili, 'when very dim people start giving me advice.'

64

I wondered, with some amusement, whether she meant me. But she went on.

'Monica does it,' she said. 'Monica's always passing round advice like cucumber sandwiches. Awful, homespun advice. I find it entertaining. Bird-brained old Monica holding forth on world affairs! It's as though the canary had started spouting Carlyle. Very boring stuff, but the circumstance is remarkable. I suppose very stupid people are too stupid to know they're stupid.'

I wanted to tell her that human kind should think more of the skeleton and less of the drapery, but I thought she probably knew that already, even if she hadn't put the knowledge into words. Anyway, I couldn't be bothered. I worried sometimes that there was something I should have done or said before I took it to the grave, beyond reach, but I was no prophet and had no real desire to be one. I must have said something about death, for Lili said, 'People used to die so easily. People in novels. Women especially. Their dear one would leave them, or they'd renounce him for some high-minded reason, and before you could say blood tonic they'd dropped dead. For a while they would grow pale and they would flutter about for a bit and then die.'

'They probably had TB,' I said. 'And they were almost certainly undernourished. Invalids used to be given food we should consider most unsuitable.'

'And people bled them,' said Lili. 'And in my opinion they were already severely anaemic.'

'I wonder if Margaret's anaemic,' I said.

'My mother used to give me iron tonic whenever it got really hot,' said Lili. 'My father's sisters used to laugh at her, but they had very strange medicines of their own – they used to have a kind of competition to see who could stuff me full of the most medicine. I was a crafty little girl. I used to spit it out when they turned round for a lump of *loukoum* to take the taste away. Otherwise I imagine they'd have poisoned me before I was twelve. Pills, potions, suppositories, ointments – they were always experimenting. They'd get the doctor to give them a bottle of something. Then they'd add to it – minced up Spanish Fly was one of their favourite things, but luckily I think they only put it in ointment. They were always boiling oil and mutton fat and messing about with attar-of-roses. I suppose they were bored stiff.'

'Your mother was the English one?' I asked.

'Mmm,' said Lili. 'How funny you should say that. They called her that. The English one. And they used to laugh at her, only she was English enough not to notice. And anyway I don't think she was quite all there. Whether she started out a bit wanting, or living with my aunts drove her mad, I don't know. She certainly made more sense when we moved to a place of our own, only then I think my father felt cheated. He was used to dozens of women fussing round him.'

'It sounds as though you had an interesting childhood,' I remarked conventionally, looking back to my brief visit to Egypt and trying to remember whether I'd met Lili's parents. We had met a great many people in a short space of time and I found it difficult to differentiate between them.

'It's interesting now,' said Lili, 'interesting to look back on, but I'm not sure it was much fun at the time. I remember being too hot. I don't really feel the heat so much now, but I remember trying to sleep on the roof under a mosquito net and still being too hot...'

'Do you remember the flowers?' I asked. It was the

66

flowers of childhood that I remembered – wild on the heath and along the lanes, cultivated in my aunts' garden, and I never knew which I preferred. There was always a thrill in finding a growing flower: the thrill of coming across contraband with the harebells and heather, primroses, ragged robin, honeysuckle and the wild rose: the calmer but no less satisfying thrill of seeing purpose fulfilled in the tended borders of the garden – the lupins, the monkshood, the Solomon's seal, the marigolds, sweet pea, and the roses.

I said, 'I do love roses.'

Lili said, 'I remember roses – and little bright snakes. Ugh.'

I remembered suddenly that I had been given brimstone-and-treacle as a child, and I wondered why and by whom. My aunts had never thought of giving me medicine. They had left all that sort of thing to the doctor. It must have been one of the servants. I wondered just how many people *had* died at the hand of poisoners before the long arm and prying fingers of the law had brought forensic science to even the outlying farms and, presumably, to the shaded alleys of the *souks* and the darkened rooms of Nilotic villas.

'I was brought up by a lot of aunts,' I said to Lili. 'Just like you.' We had been silent for some time while I thought of brimstone-and-treacle and Lili, perhaps, thought of roses and snakes. She was chain-smoking.

'I think my aunts were crazy,' said Lili. 'Looking back, I think they managed to give the impression that it was my mother who was mad, because she was the only one, all by herself in a strange land – and of course that might have made her feel a bit deranged. But in actual fact, and not to put too fine a point on it, my father's sisters were all as mad as hatters.'

'Perhaps it was just that they seemed foreign to you,' I offered politely. 'The ways of foreigners frequently appear like a form of insanity to other people.'

'But they didn't,' said Lili. 'They couldn't have seemed foreign to me because I'd never known anything else. I didn't really think they were mad at the time, although...' she added, 'I do remember scuttling through the bazaars with the youngest one veiled up to the eyebrows, giggling her head off, and me wondering what was going on. She said she was buying henna and mud to put on her face, but now I wonder if it was some mild, medical form of poison she was looking for to upset another family member. They'd've killed an outsider who tried to harm one of them but they were always playing tricks on each other. I don't suppose they'd've poisoned anyone to death – not on purpose anyhow – but some of them put aperients in the mint tea or I'm very much mistaken.' She looked thoughtful. 'They had ways of getting their own way,' she said. 'Nothing simple like asking for what they wanted or stamping their foot – although they could do that too – but just quietly, and without referring to anyone else, they would go about getting what they wanted.'

'I think a lot of women do that,' I observed.

'My aunts had brought it to a fine art,' said Lili. 'They were all terribly rich, you know. My family. Any one of them could have had almost anything, but they couldn't live alone and grow up, so they all lived together and didn't ask for anything very much except the opportunity to score over each other and get what they wanted by devious means. Sometimes just a certain seat on the terrace in the cool of the evening would be the goal, and they would contrive the most *filigree* manoeuvres to secure it. And then they would change to

68

quoting-games, and recite bits of Racine and Baudelaire, and the others would pretend either that they knew it or that they found it inferior, and they would quote their own bits.'

'That is not unusual,' I said.

'No, I suppose not,' said Lili. 'Monica goes mad if you quote at her.'

We sat in silence again for a while until I repeated, 'I wonder if Margaret's anaemic?' Lili had earlier, in passing, expressed a desire to die. I had not wished to dwell on Lili's problems because I was preoccupied with Margaret, but now I remembered my manners.

'Never mind. Never mind Margaret. Tell me why you want to die,' I asked civilly.

'I don't any more. I've got over it,' she said. 'I just wanted to annoy Robert. He orders me about sometimes when he forgets himself, and I won't have it. The urge to irritate one's husband is not sufficient justification either for death or adultery. There has to be some more compelling motive.'

'How true,' I said pacifically.

'I never wanted children,' said Lili. 'I never really wanted to get married. I only did it because everybody was doing it. It was most unlike me to want to be one of the herd. Having children makes you inevitably one of the herd. I shan't have even one.'

'Does Robert want children?' I asked.

'Mmm,' said Lili. 'He's just realised I'm probably too old to have any now and he's disappointed.'

'Reproachful?' I asked.

'A bit,' said Lili. 'It's terribly boring.'

'Poor Robert,' I said ill-advisedly – and falsely, for I felt no real pity for him.

Lili's discontent turned to rage. 'Am I a chicken to

69

have eggs?' she enquired. 'Am I a cow to calve for my master? Am I a box for him to keep his trinkets in? Eh?'

'No, of course not,' I said.

'I am mine,' announced Lili passionately, giving herself a glancing blow on the chest.

I laughed.

'Besides,' said Lili, 'having babies is painful.

'You're quite right,' I said, and Lili said she knew she was.

*

One evening we went to a pub in the town and stayed until it closed. I had thought I would be unbearably tired but I wasn't. When we got back Syl was angry.

'Where have you been?' he asked, as though he was my mother.

'Boozing,' said Lili.

Syl opened his mouth to say something and then closed it again.

I slept well that night, not waking up in the small hours as I usually did, coming downstairs to make a cup of tea and disappointing the dog who, on seeing me, would be gripped with untimely expectations of breakfast.

Syl spoke his mind in the morning, hastily swallowing a boiled egg before setting off for work. He more or less told me not to do it again.

'For God's sake,' I said, preparing to tell him that I was a big girl now, but he shook a minatory finger at me and left in a male rage, puzzled as men always are by unexpected behaviour in their womenfolk. I had a sudden sense of pity for Margaret, but I disregarded it. Syl would look after her and she would have to accept that. Dishonesty is something that even the old are not proof against, and I wanted to believe that Margaret would be happy, for if she was not then neither would Syl be. I forced myself to believe, without considering it too closely, that this marriage would work. Selfishly I wanted only to see Syl settled before I died.

It was while Lili was there that I began to have intimations of death that I had not had before. Before, I had hoped for heaven, which I visualised as a reflection of childhood – the better part of childhood, when I had recovered from the loss of my mother in the love of her brethren. I had appreciated that love very greatly because I felt that, in a sense, I had no absolute right to it. It came as a gift, not perhaps undeserved but unexpected. I missed it now that I was even older than my aunts and uncles had ever been.

Now I sometimes felt close to another mode of being, another reality: something which gleamed spasmo-dically, diamond bright, just beyond comprehension: something ecstatic and infinitely desirable, a swift, shining glimpse of unimaginable joy. I construed these visions – with the optimism which seems ultimately inseparable from the human condition – as promises, as samples of something yet to come, and, with the greed which also seems inseparable from humanity, I yearned for more. I seemed sometimes to move near to realms where the temporal, the finite, began to end, where eagles might clash with angels and the ice-bright light, shattered like gems, would scatter and dissipate until my soul could see it: low down, and far, and waiting. I admitted to myself that it could be imaginary, or possibly pathological, a symptom of age and decay, but this reasonable view failed to convince and therefore destroy my belief. It gave me not so much comfort as delight, unexpected as it was. I linked the experience in a tenuous way with Lili. I could perceive in her very little that gave evidence of spirituality. She never caused me to think of heaven, and I don't imagine she ever had that effect on anyone. It was something else: something about her that reminded me of those shimmering points of light. The nearest I can get to it is to think of seed packets with their garish pictures of flowers. Every now and then, if you feel receptive, they can give something of the pleasure of a sweeping field of poppies. The source of pleasure may be vulgar pastiche, but the pleasure remains. Not all our delight originates in the sublime, and because we are, after all, perhaps quite simple mechanisms we respond similarly to lesser, even to shameful, joys.

I had not understood before that happiness could make one wish for death. To be honest, I had never really thought about it, apart from hoping that the actual business of dying would not be long drawn out and disgusting. One of my aunts had thrown herself from her bed in the agonies of cancer.

This was something I had promised myself that I would one day face. I had not had too painful or distressing a life, and I felt there was much I did not understand, too much I was unaware of, or had refused to see. I had meant to think about insupportable pain. I had intended, metaphorically, to go round and round the abattoir and watch the beasts killed, because it seemed unbalanced and faintly unseemly to look only at the flower packets, ignoring the flayed mask of the pig until it turned up speckled with sweet herbs, transformed into brawn for the luncheon table. On the neighbouring farms in my youth they had killed their pigs themselves, but my middle aunt, who fainted at the sight of blood or the sound of squealing, had forbidden the practice and our pigs went to the slaughterhouse. I had hunted hares and shot pigeons, but that was long ago and I had wrapped my memories in forgetfulness. Jack used to hurry me past street accidents, and Syl had a tendency to take the morning paper to work with him when there was a particularly horrific crime running. I had thought I should make some attempt to see clearly and cope with horror before I departed this life, and in view of all I have just said it is ironic that I reacted as I did to what Lili one day told me.

*

She came in the morning and she looked tired. I remarked on this and she said she'd been up late. She clearly had something on her mind.

'Coffee?' I said.

'I'd rather have something stronger, as they say,' said Lili, 'if you don't mind.'

I took her into the sitting-room and she walked over to the window.

'Winter is getting me down,' she said.

'And you won't be here for the spring.' I opened the cupboard and peered at the bottles.

'I don't like English spring,' said Lili. 'I like a warm spring with almond and orange blossom and goats in the trees nibbling the leaves.'

'Whisky or gin?' I asked. Goats? I had heard her quite clearly but I couldn't picture a tree with goats in it.

'They climb trees in some nice warm parts of the world,' said Lili, gazing at leafless, goatless Croydon.

'I believe goats are well known for their sure-footedness,' I said with tea-time, drawing-room politeness.

73

'They have golden devil's eyes,' said Lili, 'and they look down at you as you go by and they look clever, and you think how astonishing they are to be clever like that *and* be able to climb trees. Then they start chewing again and that makes them look stupid, and you think what on earth are those dumb animals doing up that tree?'

'I find some people like that,' I said. 'Many people. I can never decide whether they're highly intelligent and disguising the fact, or purely bone-headed and trying to disguise it.'

'People. Ugh,' said Lili.

'Gin or whisky?' I asked again, as she made no move away from the window.

'I got stinking on Gin-and-It last night,' said Lili. 'I think I'll have whisky. Gin is a depressant. Did you know?'

'I believe all alcohol is said to be a depressant,' I observed.

'Not like gin,' said Lili. 'I'll never touch it again. Never.' She shuddered, took a sip of whisky and shuddered again. She sat down on the window seat and took out her cigarettes. 'What a hell of a world,' she remarked.

'Shall I make you some toast?' I offered, not really wanting to go out to the kitchen and fiddle with cutting bread.

Lili seemed to pull herself together. 'No,' she said with sudden, assumed briskness. 'I'll feel better in a minute.' She threw the whisky down her throat and held out her glass for more.

'Did you have breakfast?' I asked, sounding to myself officious and typically old. I didn't really care if she had or not, but I didn't want her to get drunk.

'No,' said Lili. 'Everybody got up late this morning,

and I sneaked out before anyone was around. Robert's gone off to the gallery, and as far as I know Monica and Margaret are still festering in bed.'

'Well, have a biscuit,' I said, 'or you'll get gastritis with all that scotch.'

'All right,' said Lili. She took a Garibaldi from the biscuit barrel and gave half to the dog in an absent-minded fashion. He sat very close to her, waiting avidly for more.

'It's not like Monica to stay in bed,' I said.

'She got drunk too,' said Lili. 'Only not as drunk as me. She told me something and so, of course, I had to tell *her* something, and now I can't remember what it was.'

I worried briefly that she might have confided her adventure with my husband, but it was unlikely and I didn't really care. I wasn't really interested in what Monica had told her either, but it seemed to be on her mind and she had said no more about goats.

'What did Monica tell you?' I asked.

'She told me Derek was a paedophile,' said Lili in a non-committal tone.

I wondered if I had heard her correctly. Of all the things I had thought she might say – and I hadn't really considered it – this was the least expected. To tell the truth, I had faintly imagined that Monica might have expressed some dissatisfaction with Syl. Or, if not that, she might well have let her hair down about her annoyance with Margaret, whose passivity often manifestly infuriated her.

'What did you say?' I asked, knowing quite well. My hearing was still unimpaired.

'Can I have another scotch?' asked Lili, leaning forward.

75

I poured her a large one and then put the bottle in front of her on the table.

'Derek, her husband?' I enquired idiotically.

'It's one of those things you'd rather not know,' said Lili. 'You think you want to know everything and then you realise there are some pieces of information you'd be perfectly happy without. I don't really give a damn if Derek's a child molester, only now I know the details and I wish I didn't.' She lit a cigarette and took another slug of whisky.

'Child molester,' I repeated. It never occurred to me to doubt her. Lili was no liar. She didn't need to be. On the whole things went her way in the manner that she wished; the impression she made on people without using any artifice could hardly have been improved. She liked to startle and even to shock, but she needed no recourse to fantasy. Lili was one of those to whom things happen, and one of those in whom others confide.

'She swore me to secrecy,' said Lili. 'Naturally. It's not the sort of thing you want shouted from the housetops.'

My mind, like a rabbit, hopped after a blade of imagery. I heard the *muezzin* calling between the hot clear sky and the hot dusty earth.

Lili said that Monica had discovered her husband in their daughter's bedroom in a state of some disarray. She spoke in veiled terms of something that had almost never come to my consciousness, and I knew instantly what she meant. My mind tried, and failed, to make a huge leap and get away from it.

I said, 'What?', and Lili moved in the window seat.

'I never knew,' she said. 'It never, neve. occurred to me. Clever me, who knows everything that's going on. It made me feel small, I can tell you. That's why I got drunk. I thought nothing could shock me. I thought I

76

was the clever one. Poor silly old Monica, I thought, married to that terrible bore. What a shame. And lucky me flying all round the world, having affairs with everyone in positions Monica never even heard about. And all the time...' She drank some more whisky before putting the glass down. 'And all the time... I have been in some situations, but Monica made me feel innocent. *Me.*'

I knew what she meant, for Lili was not evil, and here it was – corruption, with all its writhen subtleties of meaning. I could see her, dancing in uncertain lights, in the heat and colour of strange places, yet uncorrupt.

'I couldn't think what to say,' she said. 'I sat there with my mouth open like some big fish.'

I couldn't think what to say myself. I knew what Lili meant about preferring not to know. Such knowledge beginning with one act of wickedness leads to abysses previously unfeared because they were non-existent. Something terrible had happened and nothing was, or could be, the same any more.

'In all my life...' I began.

'I know,' said Lili. 'You've lived a long life and I've lived a rich life and we never...'

'What...' I began again, and stopped again.

The conversation went on like this for some time: unfinished questions and reflections – I suppose because we were trying to discuss the unspeakable. Besides Lili was getting drunk again.

I remembered whispered hintings when I was a girl. Table talk, stable talk – it made no difference. The whispers and the hints were the same, and also in the same category as fairy story, dark myth, or, on another level, the outpourings of the gutter press. I couldn't remember any one person murmuring obliquely of murder, bestiality, incest, and I could remember no details. It all happened, if it happened at all, in the remote farms and labourers' cottages. It was as unreal as the death of Robin Hood or the tales of the Brothers Grimm and went with the sound of the tumbling beck, the racing grasses and the darkness of a moonless moorland night. I had an impression of laughter, contempt for the primitives who could not understand that such deeds were prohibited – as much by the absurdity of their nature as by any moral considerations. The implication was that those who laughed had developed, not in virtue, but in intelligence, and those who were laughed at walked with their knuckles grazing the ground. We lived in the certain knowledge that such things happened only under other, distant roofs, and the horror was dispelled, made harmless, by half-shamed laughter, the refusal to dwell on it. Tales of darkness have always been told, but they are better told in the half dark, not in the greyness of a winter morning or under electric light.

'When...?' I asked at last.

'Ages ago,' said Lili, and I remembered the night when Monica had come, all dishevelled, without her child, to threaten hysterics in my sitting-room.

'Well...hell,' I said.

*

I couldn't sleep at all that night. I sat up in bed with a book on my lap until my back ached. The room was warm, the light soft.

I had never got used to lights hanging from the ceiling, glaring and cold. I had been brought up with oil lamps, and long before it became fashionable I had lit my present rooms with side-lights: lamps on tables, in corners. Jack used to swear and say he couldn't see what he was doing, but as he was usually only pouring a drink or looking at women's legs I couldn't see that it mattered. I sat there getting steadily angrier with Jack: with his unreasonableness, his stupidity, his habit of leaving his clothes on my dressing-table chair – the angular, mute intransigence that men could show, their cruelty.

At two o'clock I got up and went downstairs. I put the kettle on, spoke to dog and clattered the cutlery in the kitchen drawer as I looked for a teaspoon. Jack could never stand me walking about in the night. He had been a light sleeper and when he slept he liked to think that everyone else was sleeping too. Perhaps he was afraid of missing something. He had frequently shouted at me to come back to bed, to stop fooling around. I wasn't sorry he was dead, but sometimes I wished he was here so that I could tell him a few home truths I had not acquainted him with when he was alive. I didn't know Derek well enough to hate him.

I was whistling under my breath when Syl came down.

'What are you doing?' he asked.

'Standing on my head, waving my legs in the air,' I said, as I stirred the tea.

'You'll get your death of cold,' he prophesied.

'Syl, don't *fuss*,' I said. 'You're turning into a real old woman, flapping and fussing all the time.'

He didn't say anything but turned and went upstairs. I considered calling him back to say I was sorry and I didn't mean it – but then I did mean it, being very, very tired of men telling me what to do. It was unfair. Syl was not his father and he wasn't Derek, and I had no cause to be angry with him. Except that he was a man. The person I loved best in the world was a man, and I had no reason in the world to love men at all. I had been used to thinking of Syl as my son, not as a man, but there it was. He undeniably was one. And therefore, I thought hopelessly, standing up and sipping my tea, he was alien. I had learned to understand men quite well, out of a sense of self-preservation as much as of interest, and while I had known some with minds as subtle as any woman's, I had found them on the whole to be predictable. I had heard my aunts say scornfully, 'Men are all alike.' I thought as I stood in the kitchen, drinking my tea, that men were like machines designed to destroy and kill, and that paradoxically only the best of them were able to deny that tragic destiny; that good and gentle men were aberrations, a sport of nature, stopping short of apotheosis. These are the thoughts that come at two o'clock in the morning, but I do not think they would have come to me then if Lili hadn't told me about Derek.

I poured myself another cup of tea and sat down to think about Derek. Dull, ordinary Derek. Faithless, poor Derek with a young second family to maintain. Grey, aggrieved Derek. Derek and Monica. Derek and... I had forgotten the name of his second wife. Derek and Margaret. As soon as this conjunction came into my head I moved to ruin it. I put between them a vast hedge of thorns, a cold ocean, walls, rivers. They were no longer father and daughter but strangers, as distant as my tired mind could make them. I became aware of a weary rage as I realised that Margaret was spoiled in my eyes. If he had merely beaten her I would have felt pity, but she had been defiled and I felt some disgust for her. There was nothing I could do about it. When the dog had peed on a blameless cushion I had thrown it away.

Tomorrow morning I would see the priest.

But the following morning I didn't want to see anybody. Syl called in at my bedroom before he went to work and said something disagreeable about how tired I looked and how it served me right.

I had a spurt of temper and shouted after him, '*Men*', the shortest term of disapprobation I know. He could, I suppose, have riposted with as much justice, '*Women*', but he didn't.

I thought about women as I struggled to be fair to my son and all his kind. I had known bad, boring, selfish and destructive women, but they seemed to me to be as much of an aberration as kindly men. I had been born in the last century when it was customary to regard Woman as the Angel in the Home, and while I had always imagined myself to be proof against this strange idea it now seemed that it had seeped irremovably into my consciousness. My grandfather had been distant and authoritarian and I had scarcely ever seen him. His children, imperceptibly rebelling against his coldness, had done nothing outrageous (I except my mother) but had devoted themselves to being happy. My uncles (I know nothing of what they were like with their women) had been uncritical of me, warm and wide and generous, and my aunts had made me laugh and given me their cast-off dresses and handbags. They would have bought me new clothes, but I never saw anything in a shop as elegant as the clothes my aunts wore. If I had never married or fallen in love, if my uncles were all I had ever known of masculinity, I should have had a different, a positive and loving view of men. Or was I idealising them after all this time? They might have been dreadful in bed or the market-place but they were unfailingly good to me – because, I now understood, they had very largely left me alone. The words 'meddling' and 'interfering' are bad enough without their sexual connotations and my uncles were splendidly free of these traits. All day they did whatever it was they were doing – mostly in the fresh air – and they came home in the evenings, not tired and disgruntled, but elated and ready for a drink. And they'd laugh and they were witty. I don't remember ever seeing one of them in a sulk, even when he'd lost a bet. They bet on anything and everything – raindrops on the window pane, which bird would fly first from the eaves, the colour of the emergent crocuses – and I wonder now whether betting isn't healthful for men, channelling their need to take risks on to less dangerous tracks. It certainly occupies their minds.

*

I have wasted all this time thinking about men when I intended to think about women. Mrs Raffald came looking for me when she arrived at 9 o'clock.

'You not well?' she asked.

'Bit tired,' I said.

She moved over and closed the window, which I always left open a crack at night, and then stood for a moment looking down into the garden. She was a good-looking woman with strong, clear features and I'd never noticed it before. Or, if I had, it hadn't seemed of any significance. I had shrunk to being the sort of person who thinks the face of the servant of no consequence.

'You look well,' I said.

She was unsurprised and I thought perhaps her family and friends complimented her all the time and

82

gave her such confidence that she didn't mind cleaning other people's houses.

'Just had my hair done,' she said.

I lay back on the pillows and closed my eyes. After a while I heard her clanking a bucket and mop down in the hallway. She was one sort of woman, competent, sure of herself: not unlike me. Margaret, I had thought, was not unlike me, and sometimes I had thought I detected a similarity, a fellow feeling in Lili. The world seemed suddenly full of women who were nothing like each other but all a little like me. Monica, I assured myself, was nothing like me. Nor was Mrs Trevelyan.

What a ridiculous way to spend a morning. I got out of bed and dressed slowly, thinking deliberately about the evening meal I should soon start preparing. Celery soup, fish pie, apple tart with oven-baked custard. Simple undemanding food. Unexciting compared with the game and the poultry and the haunches and hams and sirloins, the great mounds of vegetables from the kitchen garden...

'Oh *shut* up,' I said to myself aloud. I found it increasingly disconcerting that I had forgotten, or chosen not to remember, the greater part of my life in favour of those early days.

Mrs Raffald, whisking a duster down the banisters, looked faintly startled.

'I've taken to talking to myself,' I explained.

'Better company than some round here,' she said. 'You'll get more sense than up the road.'

'How are they?' I asked.

'Flapping away,' said Mrs Raffald, flapping her duster as though by way of illustration. 'You'd think there'd never been a wedding before.'

'I wouldn't care if there never was another one,' I

said. I made coffee to see if it would wake me up and make me feel more alert.

'I'll peel the spuds for you,' said Mrs Raffald. 'Why don't you eat something?'

'I'm not hungry,' I said. 'I'll do the pastry for the tart and then I'll start the soup and then I won't have to do anything more until supper time.'

'You do too much,' said Mrs Raffald.

'I do hardly anything,' I said, but I knew what she meant. She meant I was too old to do anything.

'You have to keep going,' she said, 'but you ought to rest. You worry too much too.'

I considered this, wondering what would constitute a suitable, a reasonable, degree of worry. 'I don't really,' I said, knowing that somewhere in her mind was the reflection that if she had a son of Syl's age who proposed to marry a Margaret she would be worried to death.

'It's all right,' I said. 'Everything will be all right in the end.'

'Of course,' said Mrs Raffald.

*

The front door bell rang, an unusual happening in the mornings: all the tradesmen went round to the back and called out to announce their presence.

'I'll go,' said Mrs Raffald, dropping a half-peeled potato. I picked it up and finished peeling it before she came back. 'It's Robert,' she said.

'Who?' I asked.

'Lili's husband,' she said. 'I've put him in the sitting-room.'

'What can he want at this time?' I dried my hands and

went from the companionable kitchen to see what Robert wanted. He had come one evening with the rest of them but we had hardly spoken. He had looked harrassed and rather ill and not as I remembered him. I had had a feeling of unease, knowing what I knew about his wife and my husband.

'Good morning, Robert,' I said, like a polite old lady.

'How are you?' he enquired. It was a conventional enough greeting, but I was growing over-sensitive and discerned in it an unusual anxiety.

'I am exceedingly well,' I told him. 'Do sit down. Would you care for a drink?'

It was by now about ten-thirty but I was inclined to be mildly spiteful. Lili had been quite drunk by noon yesterday and had said, as she left, that she must go and collect Robert and whisk him off to lunch with his gallery owner. It would have been interesting, I thought, to have been a fly on the wall at that lunch.

'How is Lili?' I asked with a sweet-old-lady smile. I felt no animosity now towards either of them but I was sick of people.

Robert was not a subtle man. He said, 'I bumped into Syl this morning and he said you were a bit under the weather.'

I said, 'I merely stayed in bed for a few minutes longer than is customary. I was a little tired after yesterday.'

Robert looked troubled. 'About yesterday,' he said. 'What was Lili saying to you?'

I had not expected such directness. 'Why, nothing,' I said, for I would never, as long as I lived, discuss with anyone the revelation of the previous morning.

'She seemed to think she might have upset you,' said Robert.

'Did she send you here?' I asked, thinking it unlikely.

'No,' he said. 'Only she did say she wished she hadn't told you – whatever it was she did tell you.'

'Didn't she tell you what it was?' I asked.

Robert said, 'She wouldn't. Said it was nothing to do with me. She just said she wished she hadn't told you.'

'It wasn't important,' I said. 'I can't think what she could have meant. Are you sure you heard her correctly – she'd had quite a bit of scotch, you know.'

'I know,' said Robert.

'I'm sorry,' I said. 'She drank it here.'

I would have said that I had given it to her, but I hadn't really. She had mostly helped herself. For an unpleasant moment I wondered whether she had confessed her transgression with Jack, or whether she had told Robert years ago and he had known all along. At this thought I wished that I could divorce, in retrospect, my dead husband, and dissociate myself from the indignity of his behaviour.

'Perhaps you would like a cup of coffee,' I said.

'Oh, yes thanks,' said Robert annoyingly.

I warmed up the coffee while Mrs Raffald cleaned the kitchen sink and the dog mumbled a veal bone, lurking behind a table leg.

'OK?' asked Mrs Raffald.

'I can't think what he wants,' I said unguardedly. I wished he'd go away so that I could stay in the kitchen and talk to the charlady. The initial preparations in cooking, I remembered, were soothing and satisfying. It was the last-minute rush to get everything to the table while it was still hot that exhausted the hostess. I said, 'I forgot to put a damp cloth over the pastry.'

'I did it,' said Mrs Raffald. 'I haven't seen a fly yet, but you don't want it going dry.'

'No,' I said.

'Here,' she said, 'I'll carry the coffee through for you.'

Robert stood up as we came in and said good morning to Mrs Raffald.

She responded briskly, put his coffee cup beside him, thrust a biscuit at him and went out. She was invaluable. I daresay I should not have dropped his coffee over him but my hand was a little shaky again. I sat down and waited.

'Syl's looking well,' remarked Robert, swallowing some biscuit.

I was moderately glad to hear that he thought so, but it seemed an inadequate reason for his call. He could have telephoned to say so. I took a cigarette from the silver box on the table. It was stale but it gave me something to do to ward off the mild hysteria which afflicts us in uneasy social situations. If I had had some real idea of why Robert was there I could have coped, but I didn't know what he might say next, what embarrassment he might uncover. I was determined to feign ignorance if he so much as mentioned Derek. But he said very little more about anything. We conversed briefly about the falling level of the Nile – or was it rising? I can't remember. Then he left.

*

Syl came home early and I told him about Robert's visit. I said, 'I had a surprise this morning. Robert called – for no reason at all that I could see. He didn't stay long, thank goodness, but I can't think why he came in the first place.' I thought it wiser to let Syl know in case anyone mentioned it. As it turned out, I don't think anyone would have done.

'Did he mention money?' asked Syl.

'No,' I said. 'Why?'

'He tried to borrow a couple of hundred off me,' said Syl. 'So I said I'd lend him half that. He said on pain of death not to tell Lili – they're in some sort of money trouble.'

'*Money?*' I said. That had not occurred to me: the commonest, most prosaic problem of all. 'I think he must have thought that Lili had been trying to borrow money from me,' I said, looking back to the morning.

'Had she?' asked Syl.

'No,' I said. 'Not yet.'

'They're extravagant,' said Syl. 'They should have plenty to live on *and* travel a bit, but I don't know what they do with it.

*

After tea Syl went to the tennis club and I addressed myself to the problem I had been putting aside since yesterday: whether or not to tell Syl what Lili had told me; or rather, whether or not to persuade Lili to tell him, for I could not. Without knowing why, I believed that if Syl were told what had happened to Margaret he would not marry her. Pity could easily slip sideways into disgust, and either feeling was inappropriate to marriage. Almost as much as I wanted to see Syl settled, I wanted to think that Margaret could be safe. The word fell into my mind as I was trying to think of a less showy word than 'happy'. The word 'happiness' had never suited Margaret and now I supposed it never would, but she could at least be protected from further harm. Don't misunderstand me. I was not particularly fond of Margaret. My feelings were not those of a mother.

Sitting wondering what exactly my feelings were, I had a vision of Long Tom, our neighbour's gamekeeper. He shot foxes and crows and weasels so that the gentry might shoot pheasants and hares and grouse. It had always struck me as somewhat arbitrary. Since the first category of beast was already dead, why – my childish mind had asked – didn't the people eat them and let the latter category alone, free from at least some anxiety as their ancient enemies were stripped, gutted and prepared for the table? (Long Tom, I should have made clear, was a figure from my youth. Our Croydon neighbours had no call to employ gamekeepers.) Predators on the whole, being largely inedible, made poor game, although there was always, of course, the exception of the unfortunate fox, and even he, I remembered dimly, was eaten at Christmas time in some part of the world – was it Italy? There was tiger-hunting, but that was dying out as the tigers died. Parts of the tiger were supposed to have magical properties and their chopped-up whiskers were used in tea to dispatch the unwanted wives of rajahs. I knew a lot of pointless things. None of this information would ever be much good to me. It was Lili who had made me think of tigers.

Remembering this reminded me that I had known Lili much better than I had been admitting. Until the *contretemps* with Jack, I had always found her amusing, although I do not think she ever really liked me in those days. I didn't laugh very much and she needed laughter as some people need approval. She had come into my house one summer morning in what would have been a rage if she hadn't found the cause of it so funny.

'I'll tell you a story,' she had said. 'And you shall tell me what you think. Once upon a time a man was walking in the forest when he found a baby sabre-toothed tiger all by itself. No mother, no father. So he took it home and loved it and fed it and watered it and cuddled it, and sometimes he teased it and pulled its tail and tweaked its ears, and if he was mad about something he'd kick it in the stomach. And it grew up and he went on loving it and feeding it and pulling its tail and its ears and kicking it in the stomach, and all the time the tiger was thinking... What do you think the tiger was thinking?'

I said I had no idea, although I had.

'It was thinking, "One of these days he's going to go too far, and then I'm going to bite his head off." And it was watching him all the time through half-closed eyes, wondering when it could be bothered to do it.'

'Yes, it would be like that,' I said, waiting for Lili to explain that she was the sabre-toothed tiger in question and assuming that the unwary rescuer was Robert – although it need not have been. Lili always had numerous men around her, each imagining himself to be foremost in her awareness and affections.

'Men,' she said, but she calmed down and changed the subject, talked until she got bored with me and then went off in her usual swirl of skirts and I thought I could almost see tail lights glimmering on her heels. It was difficult to picture Lili in the grip of death.

The thought of death was with me most of the time. I think it always had been. Gamekeepers and death and Margaret circled in my mind, with fear – no, horror – on the periphery. Margaret was one of some protected species of bewildered creatures. Protected only to be killed... I stopped thinking like that. It led nowhere.

*

Lili and Robert went off at one point to stay with friends somewhere up North. I had a fantasy that they might pass the farmhouse, but I couldn't bear to think about it. The real farmhouse undoubtedly still existed, solid and four-square, but I did not – could not – relate it to the farmhouse in my mind, since that would be to admit that I could never return and that if I did the people I loved would not be there. You would think that time and experience would teach us not to mind, that inevitability would cease to seem like intransigence, but I have not found it so. It is not so much age as change that I have found cruel and difficult to bear. I would gladly have caught up in age to my aunts if they could have waited for me, but they had gone without me and I had had to grow old alone.

I had forgotten about Robert's exhibition, which is some indication of my state of mind. It had been in its way a memorable occasion; yet it had fallen from my memory like a fledgling from the nest, too recent and too frail to conserve. With a little effort I can relive it.

We went in Syl's car, Monica and me in the back and Margaret in the place of honour beside Syl. Margaret was as quiet as usual but seemed somehow more alive, less doughily passive. Most of the time I felt that if someone should make a thumb-print on her it would remain forever, but this evening, at least at the beginning, she showed signs of some resilience. I had dressed up for the occasion in a dark green dress and an old black velvet jacket but nobody except Syl had noticed.

He said, 'You look nice, Mum', and I told him that he too looked nice.

Margaret was pale as always, her profile in the light from the street lamps as pure as milk. She was dressed in brown, but somebody, Lili I imagine, had pinned a crimson chrysanthemum to her collar. I could smell its wintry spice from where I sat.

The gallery when we arrived seemed to me uncomfortably full. I was not a great gallery-goer, but the crowd, I felt sure, was unusually large, and everybody appeared to know everybody else, which I also felt was unusual. We were separated almost at once, and seeing an alcove with a cushioned seat I immediately laid claim to it. I was surely the oldest person present – a grimmish reflection which made me smile just a little, and only to myself. From where I sat I could not see the pictures except when a sudden movement shifted the crowd and I could catch a glimpse of those which hung opposite. One looked faintly familiar: a painting of a villa with a broad iron gate. I had not spent long in Egypt and had visited Monica's friend Marie Claire only once, but there was something about the fall of flowers beside the gate that took me back. They had been like tiny posies rather than individual flowers – a circle of white, a circle of cream and an inner circle of pink... but perhaps all the villas had looked like that, with a flow of blossoms to prove that not all was dust.

Syl brought me a glass of wine and asked if I was all right. I said I was perfectly fine and that he should go and look at the pictures and talk to the people.

Lili was talking. I could hear her voice above the others somewhere to my right, but not what she was saying. There was no sign of Margaret or Monica. I supposed they were caught up in the crush.

After a while I got to my feet and with some difficulty made my way around to give an appearance of appreciating art. The paintings were innocuous, some rather charming, but I would not have chosen to hang any of them on my walls. I gazed at a representation of the Nile and then moved on, and as I came level with Margaret she seemed, not precisely to stagger, but to droop. I reached out my arms to hold her but Robert was before me. She now looked whiter than milk, as white as ice, and her eyes were blank. Her mother pushed her way through to where Robert supported her failing daughter, and she wore a look of exasperation beyond endurance.

'What *is* wrong with you, Margaret?' she said: not 'What's wrong with you, Margaret?' with the accent in the normal place, very slightly on the 'wrong', but 'What *is* wrong with you?' which has connotations almost diametrically opposed to the expression of concern. Monica was not concerned, but enraged.

I moved to shield Margaret, but this time Lili was before me and Margaret clung to her. Syl had appeared by now and I saw with regret that he too was displeased. I had long ceased to expect much understanding from men but I had thought Syl was different. In the past he had shown great tenderness towards Margaret and had spoken of her with what had sounded to my ears like love. Now he sounded annoyed. I felt a nervous compulsion to demand 'What *is* wrong with you, Syl?' but suppressed it.

He said, 'I'll take her home', as though she was the dog and not to be consulted, or an inanimate bag of shopping.

'How kind of you,' said Lili, and that was the last thing I heard her say that evening.

She disappeared without another word and I was left with Monica and Robert in the slowly emptying gallery. I worried for a while about Margaret and how Syl might be treating her, but these considerations were super-seded by simple social embarrassment. It seemed a table had been booked at a restaurant for six of us and the gallery owner. We were now down to three and the gallery owner, and he, for one, was angry about it.

We walked to this restaurant, which fortunately was not far. The waiters, infected by the general air of disaffection and resentment, snatched away the super-fluous covers from the table and pushed aside three unnecessary chairs. I decided that regardless of my age I should have to get just sufficiently drunk to cope with all this without screaming. As a result I do not have a very clear recollection of the rest of the meal. I wondered whether Lili had gone home to look after Margaret or whether she had gone with her *louche* friends to some smoky, moderately riotous club. On the whole I thought that was more likely. Monica sat opposite the gallery owner and talked at him, Lord knows what about. Once or twice she laughed, put her arms on the table and leaned towards him. I took no interest in what she was saying, fuddled as I was with wine and weariness. I remember telling myself it was decent of her to make an effort – and uncharacteristic. With drunken charity I reflected that Monica had some good in her and was proving it by trying to salvage a scrap of conviviality out of what was, after all, Robert's evening. I tried a little as well, saying how much I had liked the water-colours, especially the one with the ruin.

*

I saw no sign of Syl when I finally got home. His coat was not in the hall. Robert walked with me to the front door while Monica sat slumped in the car, largely silent as she had been all the way back.

'Thank heaven for that,' I said more or less involuntarily as I stepped into my own house. Base-camp, even if it is not your heart's home, is infinitely preferable to wandering in uncharted territory looking at pictures.

I was so relieved I said, 'Would you like a drink?', in an access of grateful generosity, which I regretted as Robert said that he would. He said he'd go and see whether Monica wanted to come in too, or whether he should walk to her gate with her.

'Go home, Monica,' I implored under my breath, but she came in, puffy-eyed with tiredness, and her feet clearly causing her some discomfort. It must have been nearly midnight.

'Can I pour you a drink?' said Robert, who had made like a homing pigeon for where the scotch stood on a table.

'Just martini for me,' said Monica.

I was getting my second wind. If I had gone to bed at my normal time my body would now be preparing itself to wake and put me through the rest of a sleepless night. I thought I might as well make the most of it. 'Whisky,' I said, and I lit a cigarette.

'I do think that was too bad of Lili,' said Monica when she had downed her first martini. 'She might've made the effort, I *do* think.'

'I think so too,' said Robert. 'But you know Lili.'

'I don't know why you let her get away with it,' said Monica.

I thought that an extremely irritating remark and was reassured to hear Robert respond mildly, since I could not have endured an argument after the tensions of the dinner table.

'You know Lili,' he said again. 'She does as she pleases.'

Monica settled herself lower in her chair, looking as though she had just said 'Huh', which in fact she hadn't. Possibly she wished she hadn't spoken of Lili.

There was something strange in the atmosphere, something unusual. We were an ill-assorted threesome gathered together at an ill-chosen time. The only parallel I could think of was Christmas mornings long, long ago when I had risen before the sun, gone downstairs by lamp and candlelight while my aunts and uncles still slept, looked through my presents bedecked with holly, and joined the cowmen in the down-house, drinking tea and eating bread and butter with a full and glorious day ahead. This occasion felt a little the same in kind but black where the other had been white.

'I had the impression the opening was a great success,' I said, hauling myself out of the realms of introspection and fantasy.

'Yes,' said Robert, 'I believe it was. That should please the owner.'

'I thought he was charming,' said Monica. 'I don't know why you didn't ask him to come over to dinner before this.'

'I can't stand the fellow,' explained Robert simply.

I was surprised to hear that Monica had found him charming. He hadn't looked to me the sort of person to appeal to her.

'That's only because you deal with him professionally,' said Monica, making this meaningless statement in a decisive tone. 'I've asked him to the wedding. I shall send him a proper invitation tomorrow.'

By now I was fully awake and had drunk myself sober, a trick which I thought I had lost, and I could see

Robert reacting to this. Or rather I could sense his feelings from what he did not say. He was suffering the usual slight shock of those who, imagining their various sets of acquaintances to be separate and distinct, find that they have run together and the emphasis, the structure, of their social life has shifted. In a word, he was not pleased. He did not say, 'Oh what a good idea. What fun we shall all have together. Whoopee.' He didn't say anything. He was probably wondering how to put the kibosh on the whole thing.

I felt sorry for him. 'But the gallery owner isn't family,' I said. 'We hardly know him.' I felt magnanimous uttering that 'we'.

Monica became extraordinarily annoying and began to lecture me. She said that it was unreasonable, and possibly unhealthy, to confine such celebrations as a wedding merely to close family and friends. It would make the occasion more interesting and memorable if we were to entertain those whom we wished to see for no other reason than that we found their company enjoyable. She mentioned in passing 'angels unawares', and, in fact, told me everything that I believed myself and that she, until this moment, would have dismissed as heretical nonsense. I said nothing

'Well, I guess it's time for bed,' said Robert, getting up from his chair.

Monica by now was also fully awake and charged with energy. 'Come on then,' she said, 'we can go through the gardens and get a breath of fresh air.'

Now I do not fully know why I said what I did then, except that Syl was not home and I didn't know where Lili was. Until that second I had had no suspicion, no hint of a thought, about it, but there came into my mind an image of Monica's blasted summer-house, and I said,

'You can't go through the garden. Mine is complete mud and I've just laid down new lawn seeds.' Thank God Monica's interest in gardening was confined to a few pot plants or she would have known that this was an odd time for such an exercise.

'We'll go by the road,' said Robert very firmly, and I wondered what was in *his* mind. I have no idea to this day whether my alarm was justified.

I was getting tired again. I made the dog a small dish of biscuits and milk and felt that I was truly back. Not back where I belonged, but just back – back where I had to be; and on that thought I went to bed, leaving the green dress and the black jacket on a chair for Mrs Raffald to hang up in the morning.

*

Mrs Raffald came on a Saturday as a matter of course to help me put all in order for Sunday, and since she was so near anyway she had agreed to go to Monica for as long as she had guests, that is until the wedding was over. She came in at midday and announced that things were going from bad to worse at The Oaks.

'Could I get into the lounge to clear up?' she enquired rhetorically. 'No, I couldn't. Lili was in there with her feet up, and Robert roaming round like a bear with a sore head.'

'He got to bed late last night,' I explained. 'So did I. We went to his show opening.'

'I know,' she said. 'He was going on about his late night and she was going on about her hangover and Margaret's mum was going on at Margaret and Margaret was sitting there like a dying duck in a thunderstorm. The honeymoon's off,' she added.

98

'What?' I said. I hadn't seen Syl all day and had assumed he had gone to the club, as he did most Saturdays. 'Is Syl round there?' I asked. It was ridiculous to worry about a man of Syl's age, but I still liked to know his whereabouts. 'What do you mean – the honeymoon's off?' I asked as I gathered the full import of her words.

'Yes, he's round there,' said Mrs Raffald. 'They're all fussing round that poor girl, driving her mad, I should think. Not Syl,' she said as an afterthought, remembering that I was his mother.

'He does fuss a bit,' I said tiredly. 'He means well.' I knew she would be thinking that this was unmanly of him and was too polite to say so. Even in a relationship as unusually frank as ours there were certain things not to be said. 'The honeymoon,' I reminded her.

'They'll kill me if they knew I've told you,' she said, and I assured her that they wouldn't know.

'Just tell me quickly,' I said, 'so that I know what to expect. Sit down and tell me.'

'Well, let's go in the kitchen,' she said, 'and have a cup of tea in comfort.' I knew what she meant. The kitchen was the place for confidences.

'Margaret nearly fainted last night,' I told her. 'At the opening. It was very hot and stuffy...'

'Was that it?' she said. 'They were all going on about her health this and her health that and she was getting paler and paler, and then Lili said it was mad to go to Egypt because there was disease out there...'

'Did Lili say that?' I asked.

'Yes,' said Mrs Raffald, 'and then Margaret said she'd rather go to the seaside. I didn't hear it all. I was trying to polish the hall. Fat chance with everyone going backwards and forwards all over the place.'

'Probably just as well,' I said. 'It's a tiring journey to Egypt, never mind the heat when you get there.'

'Did you feed the dog?' she asked. He was trying to scratch something out from under the cupboard, his claws scrabbling and his eyes brimming with anxious desire.

'What's he after?' I wondered aloud. 'Mouse? Beetles?'

'Not in *my* kitchen,' said Mrs Raffald jocularly. She got down beside him on her hands and knees and also scrabbled. 'Bit of biscuit,' she announced after a moment. 'Wasn't there yesterday.'

'Syl bribes him not to yap when he comes in late,' I explained.

'Cufflink here too,' she said, and for some reason I said that Syl had lost it days ago and had been looking everywhere for it.

'Wasn't here yesterday,' she said, and was as satisfied as I to change the subject, for she prided herself on her meticulous housework.

'They're off to Scotland this week,' she said. 'Lili and Robert. Give me a chance to get the place cleaned up properly.'

*

Syl drove me to Mass the following morning. Monica was not what is known as a regular church-goer, but Margaret was. When Syl had first become interested in her he had suggested that he should take her to Mass each Sunday as he took me, and she had refused. I can see her now, standing in the hallway, saying with completely unexpected determination that she pre-ferred to walk. Syl had been taken aback and made

100

some joke about her being right – one didn't go up Calvary in a Rolls. She hadn't laughed.

We arrived before the previous Mass was finished. Syl went off to the club since he also was not an ardent church-goer, considering it sufficient to make his Easter Duties and turn up at Midnight Mass, and I sat down near the back.

Margaret was kneeling at the end of a pew a few rows in front of me to my left, a black lace chapel veil over her shiny hair, her head bowed. I watched her as the priest said *Ite missa est*. She raised her head to look at the altar and slowly got up, genuflected and walked up the aisle. She didn't see me and I got the impression that she didn't see anything. She was half smiling. She was rapt. It was cold in the church. I tried in my imagination to clothe her in bridal garments, to see her treading that same path down the aisle, misted in white, radiant with flowers, leaning on Syl's arm. I couldn't. Hell, I said in my mind, and didn't even feel it necessary to apologise, for something was wrong. The next Mass passed more or less without me as I strove to imagine Margaret's wedding. Hats and bridesmaids and sponge-bag trousers. Confetti and old shoes. Laughter and tears. Oh God. The awful banality of weddings oppressed me, and I could not people the church where I sat with the appropriate gathering of cheerful guests. Blasphemous reflections had assailed me as the bell rang three times for the Host, for it had just occurred to me that the bride's father would give her away – and Derek was the bride's father. I sat lost in cruel abstraction as the congregation stood for the gospel, knelt for the consecration. Up, down, up, down. My age excused my sitting throughout the service, but I felt I would need absolution to reconcile myself to the Lord after the

101

thoughts I had entertained during his feast.

Syl was waiting for me outside although I had told him, as I always did, that I could easily get the bus, which passed the end of our private road, but he insisted that as long as the winter lasted he would collect me. In the spring he feared it might rain on me. In summer he mistrusted the heat, in autumn he would say there was already a nip in the air. He was a good son.

'Lili and Robert are going away this week,' I told him in the car. 'Why don't you take Margaret and me out for lunch one day.'

'Would you like that?' asked Syl, surprised. I had refused on many occasions to join them on some expedition, wondering whether Syl was alone among the sons of men in wishing to take his mother out on trips with his fiancée.

'I think it would be nice,' I lied. My misgivings about this marriage had been increasing daily. Margaret's white, spellbound face as she turned from the altar had made my heart sink. I had felt it give an unnatural beat and fall a little. It was none of my business, but I was going to make it so: at least to the extent of trying to discover what Margaret truly felt about her wedding, and about Syl. I thought I could not bear to see him rejected and hurt again, but no man could live with a woman who wore that terrible look as she turned from the altar. *Noli me tangere.*

'We could go out to a pub in the country. Take dog and let him chase cats in the forecourt.'

'Dog is past chasing anything,' said Syl.

'He dreams about it,' I said. 'He lies on his side, twitching and chasing dream cats up dream trees. We'll give him a refresher course so he can dream new dreams.'

102

'New dreams,' said Syl, changing gear and smiling broadly.

I pulled my hat down further over my ears and started thinking about lunch.

*

A few days later we stopped outside The Oaks and Syl went in to fetch Margaret. I sat in the back of the car with dog wondering glumly why I had ever had this stupid idea. Syl and I got on well together, all things considered. We didn't bore each other when we were alone. When I say 'bore' I mean that active, almost aggressive quality which some people have. They will, it seems, deliberately set out to bore, refusing to be quiet but telling you things you know already, and things you don't agree with, and things you don't want to know. Monica was like this when she was at her worst. The bore never understands that if he would only shut up he would cease to be boring. Nor does he care. Syl and I were content to be silent together until speech became necessary or until something struck us as worth transmitting. Margaret was not boring in this sense but her presence hung in the car like a heavy, unfamiliar odour: not unpleasant exactly, but impossible to ignore. It was distracting and strange and I could think of no way either to dispel or cope with it. She was, I think, so engrossed in her own thoughts, so remote from us that her intensity became almost palpable. She seemed to belong to another order of being. Dog was more one of us, more easy and everyday than the small girl, heavy as lead with her unexpressed concerns.

Syl whistled as he drove, a ploy that was not needed when we were alone together. I wondered how it would be if I was not there, and whether he would still need to whistle through the bleak winter countryside. I wished I had stayed at home and not had to hear his reedy response to the Jericho walls of Margaret's silence.

Suddenly she said very loudly, 'No.'

I nearly jumped out of my skin and dog whined. '*What?*' I said.

The atmosphere thinned as she spoke. She sounded quite normal. 'I am so sorry,' she said like a polite little girl, 'I was just thinking aloud.'

I knew that tone of politeness. I used it myself when I wished to dissemble. Margaret was quite as unhappy with this trip as I was. What a ridiculous waste of time and petrol when at least two of the car's passengers wished they were somewhere – anywhere – else.

Then we arrived at the pub and were able to occupy ourselves with ordering drinks and staring at the menu. Even dog had had a wasted journey, as he showed no desire to chase cats: no desire to do anything but lie by my foot, as he could have done at home. The menu was dull – Sunday dinners were all that were on offer and I grew more depressed by the minute. We went through to the restaurant and sat at a table by the window. My back was aching from sitting in the car and now my temper was growing short. Syl was relaxed by his pint of bitter and looked around him with every appearance of contentment, but Margaret was silent again. I thought – battling against the urge to shriek 'Say something, you tiresome little lump' – that I had better discuss the weather.

'It's nice here in the summer,' I remarked. We had once come here often, years ago, and it had been quite nice, but it was so no longer. The old open fires had been replaced by electric logs and there were juke-boxes

104

in the bars.

Looking around I saw that the genuine beams had been replaced by artificial ones, and wondered again what it was in the human psyche that preferred the *ersatz* to the real. My temper worsened and I vowed never to come here again.

Syl must have become aware of the new constraint in the atmosphere for he grew awkward. An assumed gaucheness was one of his methods of dealing with embarrassment, and he helped himself to the vegetable dish using his fingers.

This evidence of his anxiety briefly breached my self-control. 'For God's sake, Syl,' I snapped, 'use the spoon, can't you. You're not three any more.'

'Sorry, Mummy,' said Syl, smiling maddeningly, yet still looking unhappy.

Margaret seemed completely unaware of these family tensions. She was pushing her food around her plate and thinking of something else.

And then she suddenly said 'No' again.

It was odd and rather frightening. Even Syl was disconcerted. He said 'Yes' and forced another smile. 'What do you think of her, Mum, talking to herself?'

'I think it's the first sign of madness,' I said in as cold a tone as I could muster. I was very angry: angry with Margaret and her passivity and her sudden display of negativeness; angry with Syl and his unease and his fingers greasy from the vegetable dish; angry with dog; angry with the interior designers who had ruined a perfectly good pub; angry with my aching back and my age and myself. The trifle too, when it arrived, was disgusting. I was so angry that my sight dimmed as though with weeping. When it cleared I looked up and saw Margaret glance at Syl.

There is more to be learned from a quick glance than from a long gaze. People settling down for a good look can compose their features into a suitable mould, while with a split-second glance they can utterly give themselves away. Margaret did not only not love my son. She loathed him.

'My,' I said brightly, 'just look at those cows.'

I was no longer angry. Shock douses rage. I sat up as straight as I could, stared out of the window and gabbled, for now silence would be insupportable. I felt a coldness of pity for Margaret and of fear for Syl. I talked about the time I was chased by heifers, out with my love and his cousin, thousands of years ago it seemed. I had forgotten, forgotten it because it had once given me such pain to remember. The cousin had come to stay with my love on his father's farm. She was a little older than him, a little older than me. She had red hair and thick ankles, but she was undeniably attractive despite her feet. The heifers of the father of my love had run naughtily away out of their field up on to the moors and the three of us went to chase them back; but my love and his cousin hid from me, and I was chased by the cows. I had been brought up with cows and held them in contempt, but I was frightened then, astonished at my love's betrayal and dreadfully wounded. We were very young. The cousin went away again and my love turned back to me – it was to be many years before he finally betrayed me – but I never reconciled myself to cows.

I chattered away about heifers and their tendency to violence, but as my story was really about passion and infidelity and I left all that out it was pointless and tedious.

The marriage could not go ahead. Perhaps I should

106

argue that since Syl and Margaret were related, no matter how distantly, it would be an error; plead the Table of Affinities. As much as I didn't want to see my son married to a woman who disliked him, it was Margaret I was worried about. I had never been back to my daughter's grave. My thoughts were inchoate and disjointed. I felt powerless and aged and useless and sad. I felt the way dog looked, and no wiser.

*

When Lili returned from Scotland she came round, bringing a box of biscuits with a picture of white heather on it.

'We're going to go and see Cynthia and Derek and the little ones,' she said. 'We're going to go and check on their frocks, and look in their mouths, and count their teeth.'

I found that the name 'Derek' had the same effect on me as many much worse words – words not to be spoken in family houses. It seemed to me that Derek should have been thrown into outer darkness and the signs of his exit papered over: that he should never have lived at all, and, having done so to do what he did, should be expunged from human memory. I said, 'I don't think I'll be able to look at him.'

'He'll just look exactly the same as everyone else,' said Lili. 'A bit ugly, like most people.'

'I don't see how he can show his face,' I said.

'He's forgotten,' said Lili. 'He's justified his actions to himself. He feels guiltless.'

'And I don't see how Monica can even begin to bear to look at him.'

'She's forgotten,' said Lili. 'She's blocked it from her memory. She pretends it never happened.'

107

'And Margaret...'

'She's forgotten,' said Lili. 'She feels guilty. She's blocked it from her memory.'

'I'd like to kill him,' I said.

'He'll be sort of dead already,' said Lili. 'People who've done bad, bad things start to rot away from inside. I wouldn't be in his shoes, I must say.'

'The bible's quite comforting,' I said. '...better for him that a millstone should be tied about his neck and he should be cast into the depths of the sea...'

Lili gave a hoot of laughter. 'At the wedding,' she said, 'shall I creep up behind him and whisper those words in his ear?'

'What about his new children?' I said. I hadn't thought of them before.

Lili shrugged and said she didn't know. 'There's nothing you can do,' she said. 'If you climbed on the roof and denounced him for a child-molester Margaret wouldn't admit it and Derek and Monica would deny it with their dying breath. It isn't respectable, you see.'

'We should do something,' I protested.

'Let Cain pass by,' said Lili, 'for he belongs to God. Don't worry.'

But I did worry: not so much about the new children as about how to prevent this travesty of a wedding. I wondered if I should talk to Lili about it, but the moment didn't seem right. It would sound too much as though I didn't want my son to marry flawed goods, and while that was part of it, it certainly wasn't the whole of it, as I hope I have made clear. Perhaps all motives are always and invariably mixed. I felt increasingly useless. That night I lay awake, for I had decided that in all conscience, as a Christian, I must worry about Derek's new family.

Or rather not exactly worry about *them*, but about my own incapacity, my disinclination to interfere. That dreadful word. I thought again that there should be another, better word for it and cast around in my mind. All I could come up with was 'meddle', which is worse. There was an old medical phrase about 'minimal interference', which concept I had always applauded. I believe it was invented by some doctor as he sweated among the wounded on the battlefield and observed his colleagues enthusiastically hacking off those limbs which had not already been severed but merely damaged; probing, cauterizing, anointing and bandaging. In many cases, it seemed to him, nature, left to herself, would have made a better job of it all. I had to make many a conscious effort to return to the plight – if plight there was – of Derek's new family. Frequently I would assure myself that Derek's lapse (I clothed the unspeakable in the Sunday clothes of euphemism) was an isolated instance, a moment's madness, and that he was a harmless, rather pathetic human being, either unjustly accused or unfairly punished by the exaggerated loathing in which Lili and I – if no one else – now held him. I would decide to acquit him, and think about other things such as battlefields, and then, feeling craven and inadequate, would try and force myself to face the facts. It was astonishingly difficult. My mind wandered incorrigibly from the point while I made attempt after attempt to see and think clearly. I made myself consider again the question of interference. If you came across a brute beating a donkey or a dog what did you do? You intervened, I thought to myself. That's what you did, and it wasn't called, or regarded as, interference – except by the beater, of course. And then I began imagining this beater of animals, haranguing

109

him and snatching away his whip, soothing the cicatrices of his wounded and abused beasts. I started again. I decided to talk to Lili. She would, I felt instinctively, be of more practical use than the parish priest, who was the only other person I could think of who could be regarded as concerned in the matter. It was, after all, a question of wickedness, and sin was his business, but he was an old man and I didn't want to worry him. Then I remembered that he was certainly younger than me, and went off to make myself a cup of tea.

The wedding was so close. It seemed an inappropriate time to accuse the father of the bride of nameless crimes. I grew even more cowardly and began to consider the quality of bravery. Mrs Raffald was brave. I wished I could tell her about it, but the prospect reminded me of something my love had once done. He had shot a fox (in my part of the country it was usual to shoot foxes) and had brought it to my uncles' farmhouse. I was alone and he had said, 'Come with me while I do this', and we had gone into a corner of the barn and there by lamplight he had skinned the fox and cut off its feet. I had thought it would be pleasure to be with my love in the lamplight, alone with the smell of hay and the lamp reek, but it had been some time before I wanted to be alone with him again. If, I thought, I should put this corrupt matter between myself and Mrs Raffald it would change, if it did not spoil, our friendship. It was a matter for professionals, for slaughterers and undertakers, doctors and priests, this little matter of decay and destruction. It was for others to intervene between Derek and his possible victims. But who knew? The problem was impossible. In the end I did nothing: one more cause of shame to add to a lifetime's roll of those things which I ought to have done.

*

Syl came home one evening earlier than I had expected.
I was tired after all the recent gadding about and had
promised myself an evening of solitude by the fire. I was
beginning to realise how much I now appreciated
warmth and to wonder when I had begun to do so.
Time had once passed slowly, each year like a drop of
blood from a new, as yet unrealised, unfelt wound. Now
the years flowed, clustered, congealed, and the wound
was clearly mortal.

'You're back early,' I said, too tired to regret the
reproach implicit in these words.

Syl looked tired as well.

'I thought you were dining in the city,' I said,
maternal feeling compelling me to some show of
interest.

'Decided against it,' said Syl. He had brought in a flat
parcel and put it down on the sofa. Since he was silent
and obviously upset by something, I had to make a
further effort.

'What's in the parcel?' I enquired, as if I cared.

'It's my wedding present to the bride,' said Syl in an
offhand tone. I expected him to go up to his room since
he was in that sort of mood, but he walked over to the
fire and stood looking down at it.

'Oh, what is it?' I asked doggedly. Dog lay at my feet.

'I'll show you if you like,' said Syl.

I could see his mood beginning to thaw. His pleasure
over the present was dissipating the annoyance some
setback had caused him. He undid string, unfolded
paper and produced a framed painting, holding it at
arm's length. It was one of Robert's pictures that I had
seen at the exhibition.

'Oh, she'll love that,' I said.

'It'll go just opposite the bed,' said Syl, looking at it carefully.

'I'm sure she'll be pleased with it,' I said, in as bright a tone as I could contrive. Syl was now quite cheerful and inclined to sit down and talk, but I had nothing to say that evening and went early to bed. I sat reading for a while and wondering whether Syl had taken the painting in exchange for the money he had lent Robert. It was none of my business.

*

'I won't half be glad when this wedding's over,' said Mrs Raffald. 'I can't get on with anything in that house.'

'Is Margaret still going round like a dying duck in a thunderstorm?' I asked.

'There's something not right with that girl,' she announced, stuffing a duster in her apron pocket. 'Sometimes I think she's not all there.'

'I wonder if she's ill,' I mused, remembering countrywomen's talk of green sickness and trying to remember what they'd meant by it.

'She's always thinking of something else,' said Mrs Raffald. 'Miles away.'

I wondered where she went, and then something connected in my mind. There had been a thunderstorm that night when Monica had come round, distraught, with her hair flying, but I had not previously associated it with Mrs Raffald's dying duck. I heard myself saying 'Ah.'

'Eh?' said Mrs Raffald.

It had sounded even to me like an exclamation of pain. I said I had a twinge of rheumatism.

112

'Then get out of this kitchen and back in the warm,' said Mrs Raffald. 'Go and sit down in the sitting-room and I'll bring you a cup of tea.' She brought a plate of Lili's biscuits too, and I crumbled one in the saucer while she watched me.

'You don't look after yourself,' she said.

'Does she ever say anything...?' I began.

'Not a lot,' said Mrs Raffald. 'Robert was trying to talk to her the other morning when her mum and Lili went off. I heard Lili telling him to take her out to lunch or something but he couldn't get any change out of her. She's happiest with her own company.'

'I know,' I said. I knew that Mrs Raffald undoubtedly had views of her own about the forthcoming wedding. I was certain that she found it as incongruous as I now found it myself – inexplicable and absurd – and I wanted to talk to her about it. She was the only person in my life with whom I had anything in common at all. She was solid and unpretentious and she didn't give a damn what people thought. I forgot that I had felt myself to be like Lili and Margaret. Perhaps I was, but there was no comfort in the reflection and nothing to be gained from it. What was needed here was the middle-aged quality of common sense. As a girl I had been good and I had had some wisdom, but it had been dissipated by time. Realising that I had grown old only to grow worse, I felt an immense frustration. Impotence and a weary disinclination ever to do anything again flooded my limbs and I put the cup down before I dropped it. All I longed for was peace and an absence of all feeling: dull death with no prospect of immortality and whatever it might hold. I was too tired even to wish for happiness.

'Right,' said Mrs Raffald, 'I think it's back to bed with you.'

I found I was trembling.

'This bloody wedding,' she said. 'You've been overdoing it, gallivanting all over the place, up all night with that Lili. You're no spring chicken, you know. It'll be the death of you, this wedding.' She went on grumbling as I got back into bed.

'Mrs Raffald,' I said, 'this wedding is ridiculous.'

'I know, I know,' she said. 'Don't you worry your head about it. It'll be all right. You'll see.'

I lay against the pillows thinking how undignified the neighbours would consider my conduct and my conversation with the charwoman, and how much I valued her. Without her, I reflected, I would be insupportably lonely. I had always heard that old age was a time of loneliness and it had never perturbed me, since I had imagined that what was meant was a physical separation from one's fellows. Old people who lived alone, cut off by distance, or senility, or simple crabbedness, were lonely – not me. I had kept myself to myself from choice and I had never understood until now that loneliness was not imposed from outside but had bred and spread in me until I had become its host, and little else. I had not realised until now that I was lonely.

'My Mum overdid it,' said Mrs Raffald. 'She was always on the go until I had her to live with me.'

I had been to the funeral of Mrs Raffald's mum, but not to the baked meats afterwards. This was because in those days I had grown too far from the ways and customs of my youth and had forgotten how to appreciate people with no pretence. I had thought I would feel awkward with Mrs Raffald's relations who shouted their wares from barrows, cleaned windows and drove taxi cabs for a living. I had thought they would feel uneasy with me, but now I remembered all the time I had spent in the kitchen and the dairy with the people who belonged there and how I had belonged there too. Margaret had never known that security. She had been brought up by a shallow, ambitious and pretentious woman in a precarious, silk-lined vacuum and never really felt the earth under her feet at all. Perhaps her mother had done her as much harm as... But I didn't want to think about that.

'Perhaps she should go away for a while... Margaret...' I said.

'She's been away,' said Mrs Raffald, 'and she's come back more limp than what she went.'

*

I don't know whether it was because of what I had been told, and that I saw Margaret in a different light of my own kindling, or whether she really was changing, but whatever the reason something was different. She was drinking a lot for one thing. In those days I believe people drank more than they do now – some people anyway – and I think it was those who had got into the habit in the East. Monica, I am certain, would never have splashed around the alcohol in the way she did if she hadn't grown accustomed to a way of life in which her compatriots drank more or less all the time. I remembered from my brief stay in Egypt that even the innocent-seeming long drinks were habitually spiked with gin.

Margaret, I felt, did not drink to be sociable, nor even to get drunk, but because the drink was there on offer and she had discovered almost by mistake that it made the days seem shorter and more tolerable. If anyone had reproved her I think she would have abandoned it, but even Monica seemed to see no real harm in what she doubtless thought of as convivial drinking. I never saw Margaret stumble or laugh without reason or flushed with drink, but I saw her eyes go slightly out of focus and watched her not listening – away somewhere on her own. Once or twice I wondered where.

'What are you thinking about?' I asked her one evening – out of curiosity, not in order to make conversation.

'Oh nothing,' she said, but the smile she gave me could only be described as *mocking*, and it was very unlike Margaret's usual style. I persevered.

'I have always found it very difficult to think of nothing,' I said. 'And I believe I am not alone. I believe the ability to think of nothing can only be acquired after long years of practice – by Yogis and Sufis and people who spend all their time sitting on top of poles...' If she had been completely sober I should not have spoken like that, but I was a little annoyed. Drink is supposed to loosen the tongue, and her smile had indicated that she was certainly thinking of something.

'I mean it wasn't important,' she explained. 'It wasn't interesting.' I found her composure remarkable. She was shy and too often silent, but when she spoke she sounded assured, cool and rather frightening.

There were quite a number of people present in the bar of the golf club – a ladies' night – and God knows why I had allowed myself to be inveigled into joining them. Feeling more than ready for bed I had nevertheless been persuaded by Syl to accompany him to this festive scene. I knew Margaret was enjoying it no more than I was and I wondered if any of the revellers were. It was hard to tell. A few were happily tight, some

116

talking, but most were mute – either playing bridge or just sitting there.

'On the other hand,' I said, 'I don't think many of our fellow guests are thinking about anything much. Do you?'

She had, in politeness, to respond. 'I think some of them are thinking their frocks are too tight,' she said, her eyes on a fat woman in red.

'And I'm thinking about bed,' I said. 'Monica, is it time to go home?' She was at an adjacent table talking about weddings to another neighbour.

'It's early yet,' she said, and Syl brought Margaret another drink.

I wanted to say that she had had enough, but it was none of my business. I felt sorry for her. There was no real proof that she was bored almost to death but I knew that she was, and I wondered if she was contemplating the future with an infinity of these evenings to live through. I didn't feel that I could bear many more myself and in the nature of things I didn't really need to worry. There couldn't be all that many in store for me.

'I'm going home,' I said.

'Wait just a while,' said Syl, 'and we'll come with you.'

'There's no need,' I told him. 'I can easily go by myself.'

But Syl wouldn't hear of it, and I had to endure nearly another hour in the club house, feeling that on the whole I would rather have been set upon by footpads and summarily despatched on the path home.

I woke again soon after I had finally got to bed, perturbed by a stray half-thought, half-dream. It was to do with images, with reflection and projection, and I lay awake, teasing it out. I had never liked the woman whom Jack had seen as his wife, had never liked Jack's *me* — myself in his eyes. I had seen in his eyes the reflection of the woman he loved and I had despised her; and despised him for loving her, for I could not. I wondered what Margaret thought of the girl she saw in Syl's regard.

*

I stayed in bed the next day and didn't sleep that night.

Nevertheless I felt somewhat restored the following morning and got up early. It was mild for the time of year and I went out into the garden wondering if I would live to see the green shoots of spring flowers, not being a spring chicken myself. If I would live to see the almond blossom, a goat in its lower branches, peering down with devil's eyes... Oh, God, I'm wandering, I thought. I'd better go and make some coffee.

I was going slowly towards the back door when Lili came flying over the lawn from the path by the golf course. After a moment's doubt I had to admit I was glad to see her. I knew I would be tired out again by lunchtime, but I had to give her her due: she was good company.

'Derek's wife is awful,' she said, 'I think he must beat her. She's all quiet and silly as though she'd had the stuffing knocked out of her. And she can't cook.'

'Poor thing,' I said. The mention of Derek depressed me.

'I knew a woman like that in Egypt,' said Lili. 'I was ever so sorry for her and then her husband died in terrible agonies and it turned out she came from a family of women who were skilled in herbal medicine just like my aunts. Eating Cynthia's lunch I began to wonder if she was thinking along the same lines.'

118

'Nasty, was it?' I asked.

'Horrid,' said Lili.

'I'll make you some nice wholesome coffee to take the taste away,' I said.

'We went out to dinner that night,' said Lili, 'with the same thing in mind. I ate a lot of garlic.'

She looked at me sideways and I had the impression there was something she wanted to tell me but didn't know whether she should. I waited.

'Well,' she said after a moment, 'I should think, going by the evidence, that Derek's life is a misery and a burden to him, so that's good.'

'Bit hard on Cynthia,' I said.

'We can't be bothered with Cynthia at the moment. We've got Margaret to think about,' said Lili.

'And Syl,' I said, suddenly rebellious, for I didn't want my son plunged into a loveless marriage like Derek. No, not like Derek. Syl was nothing like Derek.

I said loudly, 'Margaret is too young for him. She is not at all mature. She isn't ready to be married.'

'I know,' said Lili, 'but what's to be done about it?'

'Speak to Monica,' I said hopelessly.

'You can't speak to Monica,' said Lili. 'She doesn't listen.'

'Then I don't know what to do. Perhaps I should speak to Syl.' I poured coffee and passed the sugar. It didn't occur to me to speak to Margaret.

'I don't think that would help,' said Lili. She had the air of someone who knew what she was talking about. 'I've skirted round it a few times but he's stubborn. *And* he's bought that picture of Robert's for a wedding present.'

I said before I could stop myself, 'I'll make him keep it whatever happens. He won't want his money back.'

'That's all right,' said Lili abstractedly. 'I'm not worrying about that. I was just thinking he does seem to have made his mind up.'

'He's made it up before,' I said, again before I could stop myself and sounding unexpectedly bitter, even to my own ears. I was glad the issue was out in the open. Perhaps relief was making me unguarded.

'It would be a disaster,' said Lili. 'Most marriages are, but this would be an *absolute* disaster.'

'Maybe...' I began.

'No *maybe* about it,' said Lili. 'It would be dreadful.'

'I was going to say,' I said, 'that maybe we should get the priest to talk to Margaret.'

Lili stirred her coffee. 'I don't know why I didn't tell you before,' she said. 'I tell most people most things without a moment's hesitation but I haven't told you this.'

'What?' I asked.

She placed her spoon carefully in her saucer before she spoke, and I remembered she had been an actress – or was it a dancer?

'Margaret wants to be a nun,' she said, putting her elbows on the table and lacing her fingers together. 'I haven't told anyone this either, but when I went to see Marie Claire just before we came away I went to the convent to see Mother Joseph too – I've known her for years – and she said she'd been sorry to see Margaret go, but she'd eat her wimple if she didn't come back. And she's no fool.'

'A nun,' I said. 'Yes, I see.' What I saw was the recollected face of my intended daughter-in-law as she turned from the Blessed Sacrament. 'Yes, I *see*,' I said again.

'There'd been some trouble,' said Lili. 'Mother Joseph

said she didn't know what it was all about but, God forgive me, I think she was lying. She knows everything that happens before it happens. Margaret wanted to get away. That silly Marie Claire wouldn't tell me either – but then she wouldn't tell me anything. She thinks I don't know she'd been having an affair with Robert.'

'Good heavens,' I said.

'Silly cow,' said Lili with some force. She offered me a cigarette and I took it. 'As if I couldn't have stopped it if I'd wanted to.'

I thought this talk of sexual misdemeanour might lead us into dangerous territory in view of Lili's liaison with my husband, although it was refreshing to be with someone who did not, for one moment, think it necessary to tone down her conversation to spare my aged sensibilities. Mrs Raffald was bread, while Lili was *croissant* – insubstantial and not altogether wholesome, but enjoyable. Despite the increased drinking, and the cigarette smoking which she had led me into, I felt more alive than I had before she returned. I brought the conversation back to the convent.

'Has Mother Joseph written to Margaret?' I asked.

'I don't know,' said Lili, 'I don't think so. They don't go out chasing postulants. She'll just wait. Marie Claire's written to Monica. She says they can't come to the wedding because she's too busy, but what she means is she doesn't want to face me. She's frightened of me.' Lili sounded smug.

'It's just as well,' I said. 'If there isn't going to be a wedding.'

'I think there'd better not be,' said Lili.

*

After she was gone I wondered briefly about her motives in saying that. Most people, for whatever reason, tended to encourage marriages, but then Lili wasn't much like most people.

*

Supper was ready for Syl when he came home. I wasn't hungry but I sat down with him at the end of the dining-room table.

'I mustn't be long,' he said, cutting up his baked mackerel. 'I'm taking Margaret's present round to her later.'

I was nervous, but after all I was his mother. I said, 'Syl, do you think this marriage is a good idea?' I thought at once I could have phrased that better, or started from a different angle or possibly have kept my mouth shut, but it was too late now.

Ominously, Syl seemed not to be surprised by my question. He drew his eyebrows together but continued eating mackerel, pouring more mustard sauce over it as he spoke.

'I'm not going to let Margaret down,' he said.

This quite flummoxed me. I don't know what I'd expected him to say, but it wasn't that.

'What do you mean?' I asked stupidly.

'I mean she's had a tough time,' said Syl, 'and I'm not going to let her be hurt any more.'

'But she's so young...' I said.

'That's just it,' said Syl. 'She needs somebody to look after her. Monica doesn't understand her, her father deserted her, she was bundled off to school and then off abroad and she needs some sort of security.'

Not a word of love, I thought, as Syl continued to

122

speak in between mouthfuls. How interesting. 'Have some cheese,' I offered, as he pushed his plate aside. 'Cheddar.'

'I haven't got time,' he said, and he went out, leaving me with my mouth open.

What was so surprising about his reaction, I thought, was its extraordinary arrogance. I found it difficult to be really angry with Syl but I heard myself saying 'Men' again, under my breath. Here was the same thing, the unquestioning assumption that in the attention of men lay the fulfilment of women.

I cleared the table and gave dog a bit of mackerel skin. It was gone, gobbled up, before I could turn.

'Dog,' I said, 'you men are all the same.'

Now I could feel an uneasy rage curdling somewhere behind my breastbone. Not with Syl: with somebody else, somebody I had almost forgotten. With my eyes closed I imagined this man standing to the left of me, and in my mind I swung out with all my strength with my left arm and felled him. Then there were other men and I moved along and I felled them all. There were tears in my eyes, and I knew what I was mourning. It was my lost virginity. This realisation brought me to what sense I had remaining to me, for after all it was rather late to worry about that now. Like one of the seal people, the mermaid or the fairy wife, I felt I had sacrificed my birthright to benefit mortal men and I yearned to return to the sea, to the lake, to my element. Three blows from a man were enough to send these mythical creatures back to the halls of their fathers, and I had put up with more than that. I went and sat down in the sitting-room and lit a cigarette. I got up, poured myself a glass of brandy and sat down again feeling dissolute.

123

Then Syl came back.
'You weren't long,' I said.
'Margaret's tired,' Syl said.
'Did she like the present?'
'Yes, I think so.'
'You don't sound very sure.'
'I'm sure. She liked it.'
I was silent, for Syl was in a bad mood.

*

I thought of King David. They used to bring him virgins
to sleep in his bed and warm his old bones. Old, cold
bones. Once, in the poor farmhouses, some farmers'
families would have only one bedroom and they would
all have to sleep together. My mind was like a
disobedient dog: it would go off without approval or
permission and roll in matters that I wished to know
nothing of. It went on sniffing and scratching at the
oubliette where the subject of incest lay concealed until I
thought I should go mad. The dairy women had held
the same biblical superstition that the young should
never lie beside the old, for their vitality would all be
drained away: they would fade and wither, while the old
would rise, rosy-cheeked, with renewed vigour and go
on living. I could not, at the moment, imagine why they
should want to. I could not, at the moment, see any
virtue in living whatsoever.

Yet another morning had come round. Life was like
some debilitating, hypnotic game composed of endless
repetition: some cosmic fruit-machine – mindless,
mechanical, like the monsters in the pub by the river.
The mere speeding succession of days was enough to
unhinge the reason. I longed to be back – at home,

124

where the days had seemed to flow, not fall in, one upon another, with a jangle and a flash, and be gone again.

I thought of telephoning Father O'Flynn, but what could I say? That I wished I was dead? He might reply that, doubtless, I soon would be, adding that my desire was sinful. That I wished I'd never lived? Even I could see that that was pointless. And it was a lie, for I had once taken great joy in life. That I must prevent my son's marriage? He would think I was a jealous, possessive old woman, for he was not the cleverest of men, our good parish priest.

I sat down, for I knew that Lili would soon be round. She could not tolerate the atmosphere in Monica's house and when she couldn't be bothered to go to town she came to me to smoke and drink my whisky. Have I said that before?

She came, sure enough: light-footed with a dancer's step, her hair like filaments of light and her skirts floating.

'I brought my homework,' she said, and sat at the kitchen table making flowers.

'What do you think would happen,' I asked, 'if I told Syl about Margaret?'

'You mean about *Derek*,' corrected Lili, her fingers busy with a curl of scarlet paper. 'I think he'd hate her, and he'd marry her and hate her more and more, and when she wept at his unkindness he would say, "Don't blame me for your unhappiness, my dear. It's your father who has done this to you. You are incurably deformed in spirit, a filthy and unnatural creature, blighted beyond redemption. There is nothing I can do to help you. Lie down and..." '

'Syl doesn't talk like that,' I said. My voice was harsh.

She put her head on one side. 'Doesn't he?' she said.

I knew that part of what she said was true. The revelation would not stop Syl from marrying Margaret. He would say that the outrage upon her made it more compelling that he should take her, and look after and protect her. Everything she said was true.

'Margaret would hate him,' I said. 'She would hate him for knowing that about her.'

'But then,' said Lili, 'on the other hand, he might never tell her what he knew. She might never know. She might never know why *he* hated *her*.'

'Are you sure,' I said, '...are you sure she doesn't remember?'

'I'm sure,' said Lili. 'Couple of weeks ago – do *you* remember – we had tea with you and on the way home she wanted to talk. She wanted to confess something. Now you know me. I *cannot* keep my mouth shut. If I keep it shut sober, I open it drunk. So I told her not to tell me. She trusts me, you see, poor little bitch. Now I think I *know* what she wanted to tell me – I gathered a lot from Marie Claire between the lines – and if she was prepared to tell me that, it wouldn't take much to make her tell me anything. No – she doesn't remember.'

'Why wouldn't you listen to her?' I asked.

'Because,' said Lili patiently, 'if it all came out, if somebody – anybody – talked about it, she'd think it was me. And she trusts me. I like being trusted. Besides,' she added with patent honesty, 'as I already knew what it was I wasn't consumed with curiosity.'

'What was it?' I asked.

'Not going to tell you,' said Lili.

'What are you making?' I asked.

'Flowers,' said Lili, 'for the wedding. For decoration. It's a secret. Don't tell.'

Without shame I felt helpless tears rolling down my

126

cheeks. 'Oh Lili,' I said.

She didn't get up, but leaned across and put her hand on mine. Her fingers were stained scarlet.

'There won't be a wedding,' she promised.

For some reason I believed her: possibly because there was nothing else I could do. I was as weak and dispirited as a new-born child exposed on a river bank. I had seen a dead kingfisher once on a river bank...

I couldn't leave it alone. 'But what can you do?' I asked. I found I was thinking of Monica, of all her preparations, the trouble and expense. She spoke of it whenever I saw her.

'It's so late,' I said. 'We've left it too late.'

'Some things,' said Lili, 'only happen at the very last minute. If you think about it everything happens at the last minute. Things don't happen before they happen, do they?'

Although I found this quite senseless her tone was reassuring. Something out of the common was called for here and Lili was unlike most of human kind. She did not feel the normal constraints of accepted behaviour. She might do anything.

I went and got a bottle of whisky to reinforce the wisp of optimism I was experiencing and poured out two glasses full.

'Wow,' said Lili, 'that's more like it.'

It was now about ten in the morning and these days one glass of whisky made me drunk. I half-consciously wanted to rearrange the pattern of life, to ride across the boundaries which separated the done from the not-done thing. I felt it would make it easier for Lili to do something which normally was not done, and getting drunk on scotch in the middle of the morning was not the accepted thing for old ladies in my environment.

127

Mrs Raffald, when she arrived, was non-committal about this scene of mild debauchery. 'Don't overdo it' was all she said.

'I'd better be off,' said Lili, gathering up her bits of paper and wire. 'I'll finish this in the summer-house.'

Summer-house. I laughed to myself and shook my head. Lili was incorrigible. Mrs Raffald made me sit, out of the way, in the drawing-room and I went to sleep. I slept a lot over the next few days and I drank a lot of scotch as well. Perhaps I should have put that in reverse order.

*

Mrs Raffald came up to my bedroom carrying a tray of breakfast things: China tea, toast, coddled egg.

'I'm not hungry,' I said. I had a headache that seemed to start at the bottom of my neck.

'There's two aspirins here,' she said, picking them out of a saucer and handing them to me. She poured water from the jug at my bedside and I got them down somehow.

'I called in at The Oaks,' she said, 'and I told her I'd come back later when they'd got things sorted out a bit. The place is full of kids now on top of everything else.'

'Kids?' I said.

'Margaret's dad's new two,' she said.

'Oh, them.' I drank some tea.

'And his new wife's brought everything bar the kitchen sink.'

'Sit down and tell me about it,' I said, with a perverse wish to wallow at second hand in the awkwardness and discomfort that I was sure now characterised The Oaks.

'She don't seem to have any luggage. She's brought

128

everything in paper bags,' said Mrs Raffald, 'and left them in the hallway.'

'Perhaps she can't afford luggage,' I said, thinking of Monica's lifestyle on alimony.

'Don't suppose she can,' said Mrs Raffald, who knew everything about the circumstances of Monica's divorce. 'Only it needn't be alligator skin. Anyone can afford a cloth hold-all.'

'I hope it won't mean too much work for you,' I said.

'I won't neglect you,' said Mrs Raffald, familiar with the weak selfishness of the aged.

'That's good,' I said. 'Hand me my top teeth and I'll smile at you.'

'Eat your toast,' she said.

*

Despite the headache I felt happier that day, more relaxed. I had made a conscious decision not to worry myself to death, since it couldn't be long before he came for me anyway. Why waste strength?

'Where's Lili?' I asked.

'I saw her going down the garden before I left,' said Mrs Raffald. 'She'll probably be along any minute.'

'Will you send her up if she comes?' I asked.

'Yeah,' said Mrs Raffald. 'Shall I tell her to bring anything up with her?'

'Cigarettes,' I said, 'and sherry. I'm not going to drink whisky *all* day long. Only when there's a wedding in the offing I do think one needs something.'

'I'll tell her to bring the dog up too. He's pining down there.' Mrs Raffald had a soft spot for dog despite the mess he made. I think she was one of those unusual folk with a genuine tenderness for the old. It's easy for most people to like babies, but the helplessness of the aged does not have the same appeal.

'Cuck-oo,' came the cry from the stairs.

'Come on in,' I said.

Lili put dog on the bed and his claws scraped at the silk counterpane.

'Put the little beast on the floor,' I said, 'and move those clothes off the chair and sit down.'

She was wearing a bright red coat and was clearly going further than my house. Underneath she wore a black jersey dress, more suitable for tea at the Ritz than a drunken morning with an old lady.

'You're going out,' I said, and I knew I sounded doleful and despised myself for it.

'I have to go and sort out finances at the gallery,' she said, 'and then on to lunch with some people, and then off to dinner with some more.'

'Well, have a nice time,' I said.

'I'd stay,' said Lili, looking at her watch, 'but I must get a move on. I *had* to get out of that house. I'll tell you all about it later...' and she was gone.

*

I drank a couple of glasses of sherry and left the bottle well in sight on the bedside table. If I was going to end up as a tippler I didn't want anyone to imagine that I was trying to hide it. Drinkers I did not mind. Secret drinkers I could not abide.

'That Lili's a bad influence on you,' said Mrs Raffald, folding a towel. 'You've hit the bottle since she turned up *and* you smoke like a chimney.'

'It's not her,' I said, 'it's the wedding.'

'This wedding's getting everybody down,' said Mrs

Raffald. 'Be glad when it's all over.'

I said I'd decided to stay in bed that day and asked her if she'd leave something cold in the dining-room for Syl's supper. She brought me up a library book I hadn't yet opened and the latest copy of the *Croydon Advertiser* and I leaned against the pillows and went back to sleep. I slept on and off for most of the day and in consequence was wide awake as darkness fell.

Syl was late. I put on my dressing-gown and went downstairs. Dog had gone down earlier and acknowledged my descent with a snuffle or two. I supposed Mrs Raffald had fed him, but I gave him a mouthful of the ham she had left for Syl.

'All alone, dog,' I said. 'All alone, you and me by the telephone.'

I was waiting for it to ring: for Syl to tell me he'd stayed late at the office, or had gone with a colleague to a restaurant. I told myself it was ludicrous to worry. If we had been an ordinary family Syl would have left me years ago and be living in his own house with his own family and I would certainly not be staring at the phone, waiting for it to ring, like a love-sick maiden. I resented having been forced into admitting to myself that our situation was not ordinary, and when the telephone did ring I picked up the receiver intending to be very short with Syl.

It wasn't Syl. It was Monica.

Taken by surprise I told the truth and said he wasn't home and I didn't know where he was.

She lied and said Margaret was missing him.

I wanted to implore her to drop the pretence, but I merely said in a conventional voice that I would leave him a message and ask him to return her call.

I knew that there were women whom Syl visited. I

131

had overheard snatches of phone calls. He had recourse to them when he had no regular girl in his life. I was irrationally sure that he had gone to one of them. Fearing the ties of marriage, the end of freedom, the anchor of domesticity, my son had gone to a whore.

'Hell,' I said, startling dog, for I had shouted. It was insane that I, at my age, should be concerned with the private life of Syl, at his age. If you shared a house with someone – no matter who – you become involved in his movements, his comings and goings, his tardiness, his moods.

'God, dog,' I said, 'I'm tired.' The grave presented itself as a most desirable property.

*

Syl came home as dawn was breaking. I turned my bedside light off and lay down for a while. It was the eve of the wedding. I looked back to my own wedding and found I remembered little about it except that I had felt, on the one hand, bilious and, on the other, determined. Rather, I supposed, as the troops had felt facing the carnage of the trenches. Warfare was one symptom of the insanity of man, and marriage was another. Only a flawed species would indulge in wholesale self-destruction, and only an insecure and uncertain species would have hit on the idea of bonding pairs of its incompatible members together for life as a means of stabilising society. Musing thus bitterly I got up and dressed. I no longer believed that the wedding would be abandoned. It was too late. I spent the day pottering about, tidying up and making my own tea since Mrs Raffald was engaged at The Oaks, helping to put everything in readiness.

132

In the evening I put on my green dress, and Syl and I walked along the road to the pre-wedding festivities. The lights were on in every room and the front door stood ajar. Monica was being particularly *grande dame* and welcomed us with more formality, combined with an assumed warmth, than was natural. She kissed my cheek and led me into the drawing-room to meet the other guests.

This fell a little flat, for Cynthia and her children were the only people present whom I hadn't met before. I had brought dog along under my coat, thinking he might ease any little awkwardnesses should the children be shy, but they were shyer of dog than of anyone. They backed away from him and clung to their mother. She, I concluded, would not permit them to approach any animal for fear of germs, or perhaps rabies.

'Go on, stroke him,' I said to the little girl, but she shook her head and cowered away.

Dog was no more forthcoming. When I sat down he got behind my feet and stayed there. I said good evening to the gallery owner who came and sat beside me, seeming relieved to get the weight off his feet, and talking quite interestingly about the gangs of Soho. Monica, hovering close, gave a little shriek as he spoke of knives and implored him to discuss something pleasanter. The conversation waned. I noticed that Robert kept well away and wondered whether the gallery owner was here to check on his investment.

Margaret was drinking too much. I knew the signs. Lili had commandeered a bottle and went around filling everyone's glass as soon as it emptied. Before we left I had a brief discussion with Cynthia about the uncleanliness of the water in foreign lands and strangled at birth Derek's desultory attempt to reminisce about the old days. I could hardly bring myself to look at him, ordinary and unexceptional as he was. I felt my throat flushing with the drink and a primaeval distaste. His presence seemed both purposeless and dangerous, like a cinder from which all visible glow has gone but which is still too hot to touch.

Pleading weariness, I left. Syl walked me home and then went off somewhere. God knows where.

*

Dog died the next morning. I found him in his basket, stiff and cold as a graven dog, and all the losses and all the deaths came back and washed over me in a flood. I forgot that death brought peace to the dead and wept uncontrollably for the anguish of the living. Syl found me on my knees, unable to rise.

'What on earth is it?' he asked and I thought he probably imagined I was weeping because he was going to marry Margaret that day. As indeed I was: amongst other things.

'Oh dog,' I wept, 'dog, dog.' I liked him now. I wanted him back, snuffling with his bad breath and his hair coming out on my skirt.

I said so, and Syl grew alarmed. He took me up to my room and said he'd send for Mrs Raffald.

I pulled myself together and said I was all right. I said he was to take dog and bury him at once – at the bottom of the garden where the crocuses would grow. He was to do it now before he put on his wedding clothes. Syl left me reluctantly, looking back over his shoulder perhaps to make sure I wouldn't die also on his wedding morning.

I went to the window and watched him walk down the garden, carrying dog and a spade. He began to dig, stopping frequently to straighten his shoulders and look around. He was probably taking deep breaths to remind himself that he still lived. He looked notably free, like a prisoner just released and I felt compunction at my ingratitude. Perhaps he was as constricted as I by our relationship. I wasn't surprised, when he had filled in dog's grave, to see him go out of the garden, along the path to Monica's summer-house, and thought he must have decided to snatch Mrs Raffald from her duties to come and minister to me. I began to dress for the wedding, not wanting to be too obvious a skeleton at the feast.

*

Breathless, Mrs Raffald came into my room.

'I'm nearly ready,' I said, trying to give an appearance of sense and decisiveness. 'You needn't have come.'

'You needn't go,' she said. 'The wedding's off.'

*

I sat on my bed feeling deader than dog, even experiencing the peace of the dead.

'You can take your hat off now,' Mrs Raffald said.

'Have I got it on?' I asked. I raised my hand to my head to make sure, and there it was: the hat I had always worn to weddings. How significant, I thought, that I hadn't bothered to buy a new hat for my son's wedding. It hadn't occurred to me before.

'What happened?' I asked, not caring. 'Where's Syl?'

I realised that I had no idea whether he'd come back

135

from interring dog to get into his wedding clothes. I said, 'I think I'm losing my grip.' I thought, I know now what that means: it means we're all at sea in a storm, clinging to the mizzen mast or the lifeboat's rim or the captain's sleeve, and one by one we tire and we loosen our grip and away we go, down to the depths.

'He went down the pub,' said Mrs Raffald.

That sounded reassuring. People didn't go down the pub to shoot themselves.

This reflection brought me back to life. The cancellation of a wedding at the last, the very last minute, was, if I remembered correctly, not a thing to be taken lightly. I struggled to accommodate myself to this idea, but I didn't want to think about it. I started to speak again but my words were slurred. I could hear them – thick, unsteady and wet round the edges. I said, 'I'm not drunk – I haven't been drinking anything', and then I thought that that was a most unseemly remark for a lady to make on the day of her son's wedding.

I began to feel better. Surely all was now well. Few of us had wanted this wedding.

'On the other hand,' I said, and now I was speaking more clearly, 'I could easily be going mad. I feel as though I am.'

'It's shock,' said Mrs Raffald.

I was conscious of myself as though I could see myself in a mirror. I could see an old woman shaking as with the palsy, putting out a tremulous hand for comfort, puzzled and fearful and at a loss.

'Then in that case,' I said, my voice still not quite right, 'we'd better have a drink.'

She went away and came back with the brandy.

I said, 'I prefer whisky usually, but I'll make do with this. Can I have a cigarette?'

She said, 'That Lili...'

I said, 'She's a bad influence isn't she?' I was feeling stronger. 'How do you know Syl went to the pub? Did he tell you?'

'I told him,' said Mrs Raffald calmly. She was a calming person. A good influence. 'I told him to go.'

Clearly something momentous must have happened – Mrs Raffald did not habitually give my son orders – but I increasingly did not care what it was. I said, 'Let's have just one more drink', and I wondered briefly what Monica would do with the baked meats – but baked meats were what you had at funerals. This was to have been a wedding. I fell asleep reflecting that while weddings could be definitely cancelled, funerals could only be postponed.

*

I never really knew exactly what had happened, although I remember Mrs Raffald uttering the word 'summer-house', and experiencing a swift, hallucinatory image: a sense of *déja vu* which would have rocked me back on my heels if I had not been sitting down. What she said, or hinted at, was not unexpected. I thought confusedly, 'I know, I know, I saw them.' Past and present were superimposed on each other, everything was repeated, nothing was new. Lili and Jack, Lili and Syl, Lili and all the devils in hell... Bless her. I never saw her again.

*

Syl refused to discuss the matter. He said there'd been a scene. They were all mad round there, and Margaret

137

herself had turned out to suffer from religious mania. He said he was going to marry Miss Benson from the office...

*

'Mrs Raffald,' I said some time later, 'did Lili...?' But I didn't really want to know. Details were unimportant and frequently distressing, and Mrs Raffald would not burden me with them. Anyway, perhaps I did know.

She said, 'I'm not saying nothing, All I'm saying is she'll never wear that hat again in public.'

And she laughed and laughed and laughed.